Published in 2016 by Britannica Educational Publishing (a trademark of Encyclopædia Britannica, Inc.) in association with The Rosen Publishing Group, Inc.
29 East 21st Street, New York, NY 10010

Copyright © 2016 The Rosen Publishing Group, Inc. and Encyclopædia Britannica, Inc. Encyclopaedia Britannica, Britannica, and the Thistle logo are registered trademarks of Encyclopædia Britannica, Inc. All rights reserved.

Rosen Publishing materials copyright © 2016 The Rosen Publishing Group, Inc. All rights reserved.

Distributed exclusively by Rosen Publishing.
To see additional Britannica Educational Publishing titles, go to rosenpublishing.com.

First Edition

Britannica Educational Publishing
J. E. Luebering: Director, Core Reference Group
Anthony L. Green: Editor, Compton's by Britannica

Rosen Publishing
Hope Lourie Killcoyne: Executive Editor
Monica K. Gill: Editor
Nelson Sá: Art Director
Brian Garvey: Designer
Cindy Reiman: Photography Manager
Karen Huang: Photo Researcher
Introduction and supplementary material by Edward Willett

Library of Congress Cataloging-in-Publication Data

Biopharmaceuticals/edited by Monica K. Gill.
    pages cm.—(The biotechnology revolution)
Audience: Grades 7–12.
Includes bibliographical references and index.
ISBN 978-1-62275-582-0 (library bound)
1. Biopharmaceutics—Juvenile literature. I. Gill, Monica K., editor.
RM301.4.B533 2016
615.7—dc23

2015000582

Manufactured in the United States of America

Photo credits: Cover, p. 1 Suwit Ngaokaew/Shutterstock.com; p. xi Imaginechina/AP Images; pp. 3, 11 Sheila Terry/Science Source; p. 5 Gerald Raab/picture-alliance/dpa/AP Images; p. 15 Print Collector/Hulton Archive/Getty Images; p. 23 Popperfoto/Getty Images; p. 27 © William J. Clinton Presidential Library; pp. 39, 48 BSIP/UIG/Getty Images; pp. 43, 69, 76, 102, 115, 118, 129 Encyclopædia Britannica, Inc.; p. 51 Inga Spence/Visuals Unlimited/Getty Images; p. 55 Dorling Kindersley/Getty Images; p. 58 Philippe Huguen/AFP/Getty Images; p. 62 Stan Wayman/The Life Picture Collection/Getty Images; p. 66 Bloomberg/Getty Images; p. 71 Jonathan A Meyers/Science Source/Getty Images; p. 85 SCIMAT/Science Source; p. 96 Watson Pharmaceuticals/AP Images; p. 105 Miguel Medina/AFP/Getty Images; p. 111 Schering-Plough/Science Source; p. 139 © Photodisc/Thinkstock; p. 143 © AP Images; p. 145 Inga Spence/Science Source; p. 148 Tom Deerinck and Mark Ellisman of the National Center for Microscopy and Imaging Research at the University of California at San Diego; p. 154 Darren Hauck/Getty Images; cover and interior design elements vitstudio/Shutterstock.com (DNA), everythingpossible/iStock/Thinkstock (honeycomb), style_TTT/Shutterstock.com (linear patterns).

CONTENTS

INTRODUCTION VIII

CHAPTER 1
THE HISTORY OF PHARMACEUTICALS 1
MEDICINES OF ANCIENT CIVILIZATIONS 2
PHARMACEUTICAL SCIENCE IN THE 16TH AND 17TH
CENTURIES 4
    PHARMACOPOEIA 6
    PHARMACOLOGY 8
ISOLATION AND SYNTHESIS OF COMPOUNDS 10
DISCOVERY OF ANTISEPTICS AND VACCINES 12
    EDWARD JENNER 14
IMPROVEMENT IN DRUG ADMINISTRATION 17
NEW CLASSES OF PHARMACEUTICALS 18
TRANSITIONS IN DRUG DISCOVERY 19
EARLY EFFORTS IN THE DEVELOPMENT OF
    ANTI-INFECTIVE DRUGS 21
DISCOVERY OF PENICILLIN 22
ISOLATION OF INSULIN 25
IDENTIFICATION OF VITAMINS 28
EMERGENCE OF MODERN DISEASES AND TREATMENT 30
    HYPERTENSION 30
    EARLY PROGRESS IN CANCER DRUG
    DEVELOPMENT 32
THE PHARMACEUTICAL INDUSTRY IN
THE MODERN ERA 33
    EMERGENCE OF THE BIOPHARMACEUTICAL
    INDUSTRY 34
    TREATING DIABETES 40

CHAPTER 2
DRUG DISCOVERY AND DEVELOPMENT 43
RESEARCH AND DISCOVERY 44
CONTRIBUTION OF SCIENTIFIC KNOWLEDGE TO DRUG DISCOVERY 45
DRUG SCREENING 47
SOURCES OF COMPOUNDS 47
LEAD CHEMICAL IDENTIFICATION 47
Taxol and the Pacific Yew 50
STRATEGIES FOR DRUG DESIGN AND PRODUCTION 53
STRUCTURE-ACTIVITY RELATIONSHIP. 54
COMPUTER-AIDED DESIGN OF DRUGS 56
COMBINATORIAL CHEMISTRY 56
SYNTHETIC HUMAN PROTEINS. 57
PERSONALIZED MEDICINE 58

CHAPTER 3
DRUG REGULATION AND APPROVAL 60
PUBLIC INFLUENCE ON DRUG REGULATION 61
OBJECTIVES AND ORGANIZATION OF DRUG REGULATORY AGENCIES 63
DRUG APPROVAL PROCESS. 64
Food and Drug Administration 66
THE INVESTIGATIONAL NEW DRUG APPLICATION. 67
THE NEW DRUG APPLICATION AND BIOLOGICS LICENSE APPLICATION. 70
SAFETY TESTING IN ANIMALS 72
PHARMACOKINETIC INVESTIGATION. 74
DOSAGE FORM DEVELOPMENT 75
Common Dosage Forms 77

OBSTACLES IN DRUG DEVELOPMENT 88
   ADVERSE REACTIONS 89
   POSTMARKETING ADVERSE DRUG EVENTS 91
   DRUG INTERACTIONS 93
   DRUG PATENTS 95

CHAPTER 4
MAJOR APPLICATIONS OF BIOPHARMACEUTICALS 98

ANTIBIOTICS 99
   USE AND ADMINISTRATION OF ANTIBIOTICS 100
   CATEGORIES OF ANTIBIOTICS 100
   ANTIBIOTIC RESISTANCE 101
   MAJOR ANTIBIOTICS 102

VACCINES 103

CYTOKINES 107
   INTERFERON 110

MONOCLONAL ANTIBODIES 109
   HYBRIDOMA 113
   HUMAN MONOCLONAL ANTIBODIES 116

CELL THERAPY 117

ENZYMES 125

HORMONES 127

BLOOD FACTORS 130

ANTISENSE DRUGS 133

PEPTIDE THERAPEUTICS 134

CHAPTER 5
THE FUTURE OF BIOPHARMACEUTICALS . . . 137

GENE THERAPY 138

PHARMACOGENETICS 138
PHARMING 141
    ATRYN 144
SYNTHETIC BIOLOGY 146
    ADVANCES IN SYNTHETIC BIOLOGY 147
    APPLICATIONS OF SYNTHETIC BIOLOGY 151
BIOETHICAL CONSIDERATIONS 152
    CONCLUSION 157
    GLOSSARY 159
    BIBLIOGRAPHY 162
    INDEX 164

INTRODUCTION

In the 21st century an astonishing variety of new drugs have been developed. In 2012 alone, the United States Food and Drug Administration (FDA) approved 39 novel new medicines, known as new molecular entities (NMEs)—the largest number in fifteen years. In all, the FDA approved more than 250 new NMEs between 2004 and 2014.

The new therapies approved in 2012 included the first that targets the underlying cause of cystic fibrosis, the first medicine approved for the treatment of the most common form of skin cancer, the first new tuberculosis medicine in 40 years, three new therapies for leukemia, and a new medicine to treat respiratory distress syndrome in premature infants.

What drove the development of these new medicines? The burgeoning field of biopharmaceuticals.

Although at present there is no precise scientific definition of a biopharmaceutical, at its most basic, a biopharmaceutical is distinguished by what it is derived from and how it is manufactured. In general, biopharmaceuticals are manufactured by biotechnology methods and involve complex biological molecules, whereas non-biopharmaceutical drugs are manufactured by chemical, nonbiological means and involve small molecules and other chemical substances.

INTRODUCTION

Because they are derived from biological systems, biopharmaceuticals are typically made up of highly complex macromolecules that may be more than 100 times larger than the molecules of more ordinary drugs like aspirin. (Aspirin has a molecular weight of 180, whereas interferon beta, a biopharmaceutical, has a molecular weight of 19,000.)

In one sense, biopharmaceuticals have existed for centuries. Traditional medicine relied largely on naturally occurring plants, and these plants were the basis for some of the earliest medicines developed in the scientific era. Indeed, scientists continue to explore some of these traditional remedies and also to study other plants in the hope of identifying promising new medicines.

One of the greatest breakthroughs in early pharmaceutical science was the discovery of the antibiotic properties of penicillin—derived from a naturally occurring mold, and thus a classic example of a biopharmaceutical. Much later, the discovery of insulin made the formerly fatal illness of diabetes a chronic, manageable condition. Insulin, too, is a biopharmaceutical, originally extracted from the pancreases of slaughtered animals, primarily cattle and pigs.

Interestingly, however, a new way to produce insulin also ushered in the modern biopharmaceutical industry, which grew out of the first use of restriction enzymes to "cut and paste" strands of deoxyribonucleic acid (DNA) in 1972. The ability to manipulate DNA directly allowed researchers to place genes for the production of complex biological molecules into bacteria, which then produced those molecules in sufficient numbers to make the technique a viable method of large-scale commercial production. Insulin produced using this "recombinant DNA technology" was approved for human use in 1982, launching the modern biopharmaceutical industry.

Other early biopharmaceuticals include somatostatin (a drug used to treat neuroendocrine tumours and acromegaly, also known as gigantism), human growth hormone, interferon gamma, and other important molecules. Like insulin, these molecules were originally obtained using animal or human tissue. Now, the ability to synthesize them in the laboratory has made production cheaper and safer. In the case of insulin, the animal-derived product was closely related to human insulin, but not an exact match, and in rare instances diabetics suffered allergic reactions to it. Recombinant DNA technology has meant that today diabetics are treated using human rather than animal insulin—good news both for patients and for the millions of animals that would otherwise have to be slaughtered to meet the demand.

INTRODUCTION

Biopharmaceuticals have provided—and hold the promise of continuing to provide— astounding advances in antibiotics and vaccines, as well as new treatments based on cytokines, monoclonal antibodies, enzymes, hormones and more. New fields of treatment like cell therapy, antisense drugs, and peptide therapeutics are opening up even more possibilities as advances continue.

Like all pharmaceuticals, biopharmaceuticals must

A worker checks eggs to be used for producing inactivated influenza A H1N1 vaccine at the plant of Sinovac Biotech Ltd., a biopharmaceutical company based in Beijing.

pass through a rigorous approval process. However, in contrast to traditional drugs, biopharmaceuticals have greater potential to cure disease rather than merely treat symptoms, and they often have fewer side effects because of their specificity—unlike synthetic drugs, biopharmaceuticals structurally mimic compounds already found within the body.

Because of the promise they hold and the success they have already demonstrated, biopharmaceuticals make up about one-third of the drugs currently in development. The exciting advances in this field have made it a vital and continuously growing part of the economy. According to figures compiled by the Pharmaceutical Research and Manufacturers of America (PhRMA), the U.S. biopharmaceutical sector employs more than 810,000 workers, supports a total of nearly 3.4 million jobs across the country, and, when direct, indirect, and induced effects are considered, contributes nearly $790 billion in economic output on an annual basis.

According to the National Science Foundation, the U.S. biopharmaceutical sector accounts for the single largest share of all U.S. business research and development, representing nearly 20 percent of all domestic research and development (R&D) funded by U.S. companies.

The major categories of biopharmaceuticals include:

- Cytokines: These hormone-like molecules

INTRODUCTION

control reactions between cells and activate cells of the immune system, such as lymphocytes and macrophages. Interferon is one example. Interferon is a glycoprotein cytokine that acts against viruses and uncontrolled cell proliferation (cancer). Interleukins are also cytokines. They are messenger molecules for various steps in the immune process.

- Enzymes: These complex proteins cause specific chemical changes in other substances without being changed themselves. An example of a biopharmaceutical enzyme is alteplase, better known as TPA, which dissolves blood clots and is used in the treatment of heart attack and stroke.
- Hormones: These chemicals transfer information and instructions between cells in living organisms. Insulin and human growth hormone are two of those so far produced by the biopharmaceutical industry.
- Clotting Factors: These include any protein in the blood essential for coagulation. Deficiencies in clotting factors produce the various forms of hemophilia. For many years human clotting factors were produced from donated plasma. In the 1970s and 1980s, the use of plasma contaminated with HIV resulted in thousands of hemophiliacs in the United States contracting AIDS. Today, almost all

human clotting factors that are produced are done so using recombinant DNA technology, eliminating the risk of contaminated blood.
- Vaccines: Vaccines are made up of microorganisms or parts of microorganisms that stimulate resistance in humans and an immune response to specific diseases. Vaccination, which began with Edward Jenner's discovery that cowpox could be used to vaccinate people against the much more dangerous disease smallpox, has been one of the great success stories of public health, and researchers continue to seek to develop new vaccines for diseases such as hepatitis B and ebola.
- Monoclonal Antibodies: Monoclonal antibodies are identical antibodies produced from cloned cells. Because all the antibodies are identical, they can be used to effectively target a specific disease. Today six out of ten of the best-selling drugs in the world are monoclonal antibody therapeutics. Humira, a monoclonal antibody treatment for rheumatoid arthritis and other autoimmune conditions, was the top-selling drug worldwide in 2012, with a revenue of $9.3 billion.
- Cell Therapies: Cell therapy is the introduction of new cells into tissues in order to treat a disease. Stem cells—cells that can be programmed to form many different kinds of

INTRODUCTION

tissue—are the usual focus of cell therapy, of which the best-known example is the transplanting of bone marrow stem cells to treat leukemia and other types of cancer, as well as various blood disorders. Scientists in this cutting-edge area of research are also exploring the use of stem cells to treat Parkinson's, celiac disease, heart failure, and many other illnesses and disorders.

- Antisense Drugs: An antisense drug is a medication that contains part of the non–coding strand of messenger RNA (mRNA). These drugs do not attack the bacteria or viruses causing a disease; rather, they disrupt the portion of the cell's genetic machinery that produces disease-causing proteins in response to the bacterial or viral infection. Antisense drugs hold promise for the treatment of cancer and various genetic disorders.
- Peptide Therapeutics: Peptides are short polymers made up of linked amino acids (usually fewer than 100). Many of the basic components of human biological processes, including enzymes, hormones, and antibodies, are made up of peptides. They get their name from the link between one amino acid residue and the next, which is known as a peptide bond. (Proteins are similarly made up of amino acids linked by peptide bonds but are typically much

longer chains of more than 100 amino acids.) Compared to other small-molecule drugs synthesized using chemical rather than biopharmaceutical processes, peptides typically offer low toxicity and high specificity. They're one of the fastest-growing areas of biopharmaceutical research, with more than 40 approved peptide-based medicines already in use today and hundreds more in development to treat everything from allergies to cancer and Alzheimer, Huntington, and Parkinson diseases.

While the field of biopharmaceuticals is both too large and too fast-growing to be covered in detail in a short text, the following pages will provide a basic overview of this exciting aspect of modern medicine. Beginning with a brief history of pharmaceuticals in general and biopharmaceuticals in particular, this volume continues with an overview of the drug discovery, development, regulation, and approval process (which is largely the same for both conventional drugs and biopharmaceutical medicines), before moving on to a more detailed look at some of the major applications of biopharmaceuticals mentioned above, then wrapping up with a peek at the future of biopharmaceuticals, including gene therapy, pharmacogenetics, pharming, and synthetic biology—and some of the ethical considerations they raise.

CHAPTER 1

THE HISTORY OF PHARMACEUTICALS

The modern era of the pharmaceutical industry—of isolation and purification of compounds, chemical synthesis, and computer-aided drug design—is considered to have begun in the 19th century, thousands of years after intuition and trial and error led humans to believe that plants, animals, and minerals contained medicinal properties. The unification of research in the 20th century in fields such as chemistry and physiology increased the understanding of basic drug-discovery processes. Identifying new drug targets, attaining regulatory approval from government agencies, and refining techniques in drug discovery and development are among the challenges that face the pharmaceutical industry today. The continual evolution and advancement of the pharmaceutical industry is fundamental in the control and elimination of disease around the world.

MEDICINES OF ANCIENT CIVILIZATIONS

The oldest records of medicinal preparations made from plants, animals, or minerals are those of the early Chinese, Hindu, and Mediterranean civilizations. An herbal compendium, said to have been written in the 28th century BCE by the legendary emperor Shennong, described the antifever capabilities of a substance known as *chang shan* (from the plant species *Dichroa febrifuga*), which has since been shown to contain antimalarial alkaloids (alkaline organic chemicals containing nitrogen). Workers at the school of alchemy that flourished in Alexandria, Egypt, in the 2nd century BCE prepared several relatively purified inorganic chemicals, including lead carbonate, arsenic, and mercury. According to *De materia medica*, written by the Greek physician Pedanius Dioscorides in the 1st century CE, verdigris (basic cupric acetate) and cupric sulfate were prescribed as medicinal agents. While attempts were made to use many of the mineral preparations as drugs, most proved to be too toxic to be used in this manner.

Many plant-derived medications employed by the ancients are still in use today. Egyptians treated constipation with senna pods and castor

THE HISTORY OF PHARMACEUTICALS

Pedanius Dioscorides, who penned De materia medica, *the leading pharmacological text for 16 centuries, is seen here receiving a mandrake plant to use as part of an anesthetic.*

oil and indigestion with peppermint and caraway. Various plants containing digitalis-like compounds (cardiac stimulants) were employed to treat a number of ailments. Ancient Chinese physicians employed ma huang, a plant containing ephedrine, for a variety of purposes. Today ephedrine is used in many pharmaceutical preparations intended for the treatment of cold and allergy symptoms. The Greek physician Galen (*c.* 130–*c.* 200 CE) included opium and squill among the drugs in his apothecary shop (pharmacy). Today derivatives of opium alkaloids are widely employed for pain relief, and, while squill was used for a time as a cardiac stimulant, it is better known as a rat poison. Although many of the medicinal preparations used by Galen are obsolete, he made many important conceptual contributions to modern medicine. For example, he was among the first practitioners to insist on purity for drugs. He also recognized the importance of using the right variety and age of botanical specimens to be used in making drugs.

PHARMACEUTICAL SCIENCE IN THE 16TH AND 17TH CENTURIES

Pharmaceutical science improved markedly in the 16th and 17th centuries. In 1546 the first pharmacopoeia, or collected list of drugs and medicinal chemicals with directions for making pharmaceutical preparations, appeared in Nürnberg, Ger. Previous to this time, medical preparations had varied in concentration and even in constituents. Other pharmacopoeias followed in Basel (1561), Augsburg (1564), and London (1618). The *London Pharmacopoeia* became mandatory for the whole of England and thus became the first example of a national pharmacopoeia. Another important advance was initiated by Paracelsus, a 16th-century

The History of Pharmaceuticals

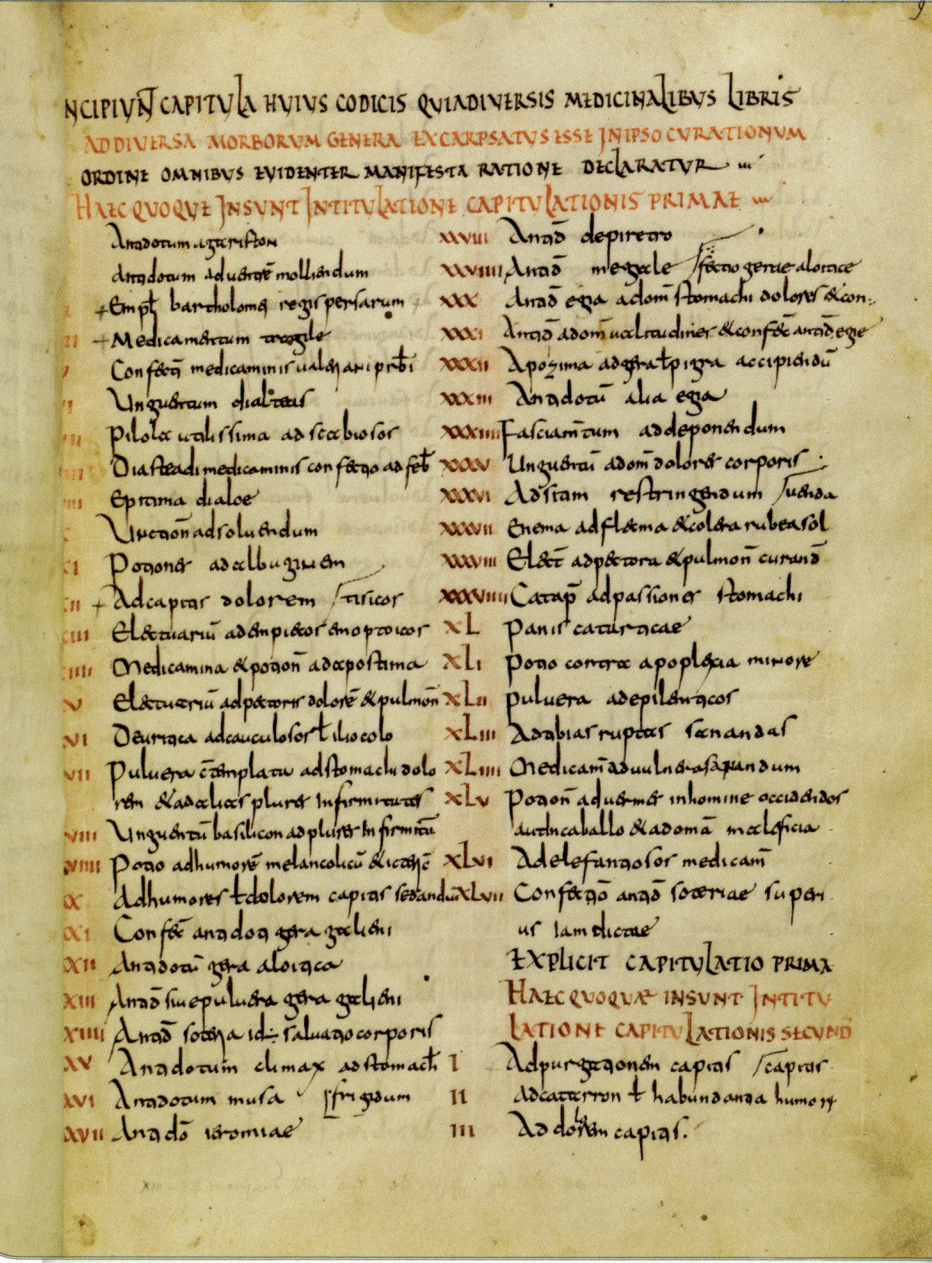

The Lorsch pharmacopoeia, written in the 8th century CE, is one of the oldest existing medical compendiums from medieval Europe.

Swiss physician-chemist. He admonished his contemporaries not to use chemistry as it had widely been employed prior to his time in the speculative science of alchemy and the making of gold. Instead, Paracelsus advocated the use of chemistry to study the preparation of medicines.

PHARMACOPOEIA

A pharmacopoeia is a book published by a government, or otherwise under official sanction, to provide standards of strength and purity for therapeutic drugs. The primary function of a pharmacopoeia is to describe the formulation of each drug on the selected list. The provisions of the pharmacopoeia are binding upon all who produce drugs and who dispense them.

The task of compiling most pharmacopoeias is carried out by experts in the professions of medicine, chemistry, and pharmacy at the request of the agency undertaking the compilation. Most programs are financed from government funds, but the *British Pharmacopoeia* and the *Pharmacopeia of the United States* are written by private, nonprofit organizations with the sanction of their respective governments. The proceeds of their sale support their revision. Most countries not having a national pharmacopoeia have adopted one of another country or countries or, in some cases, the *International Pharmacopoeia*, which was put forward by the World Health Organization in 1951 as a recommendation aimed at minimizing or eliminating variations among national pharmacopoeial standards.

In London the Society of Apothecaries (pharmacists) was founded in 1617. This marked the emergence of pharmacy as a distinct and separate entity. The separation of apothecaries from grocers was authorized by King James I, who also mandated that only a member of the society could keep an apothecary's shop and make or sell pharmaceutical preparations. In 1841 the Pharmaceutical Society of Great Britain was founded. This society oversaw the education and training of pharmacists to assure a scientific basis for the profession. Today professional societies around the world play a prominent role in supervising the education and practice of their members.

In 1783 the English physician and botanist William Withering published his famous monograph on the use of digitalis (an extract from the flowering purple foxglove, *Digitalis purpurea*). His book, *An Account of the Foxglove and Some of Its Medicinal Uses: With Practical Remarks on Dropsy and Other Diseases*, described in detail the use of digitalis preparations and included suggestions as to how their toxicity might be reduced. Plants containing digitalis-like compounds had been employed by ancient Egyptians thousands of years earlier, but their use had been erratic. Withering believed that the primary action of digitalis was on the kidney, thereby preventing dropsy (edema). Later, when it was discovered that water was transported in the circulation with blood, it was found that the primary action of digitalis was to improve cardiac

PHARMACOLOGY

Pharmacology is a branch of medicine that deals with the interaction of drugs with the systems and processes of living animals, in particular, the mechanisms of drug action as well as the therapeutic and other uses of the drug.

The first Western pharmacological treatise, a listing of herbal plants used in classical medicine, was made in the 1st century CE by the Greek physician Dioscorides. The medical discipline of pharmacology derives from the medieval apothecaries, who both prepared and prescribed drugs. In the early 19th century a split developed between apothecaries who treated patients and those whose interest was primarily in the preparation of medicinal compounds; the latter formed the basis of the developing specialty of pharmacology. A truly scientific pharmacology developed only after advances in chemistry and biology in the late 18th century enabled drugs to be standardized and purified. By the early 19th century, French and German chemists had isolated many active substances—morphine, strychnine, atropine, quinine, and many others—from their crude plant sources.

Pharmacology was firmly established in the later 19th century by the German Oswald Schmeiderberg (1838-1921). He defined its purpose, wrote a textbook of pharmacology, helped to found the first pharmacological journal, and, most importantly, headed a school at Strasbourg that became the nucleus from which independent departments of pharmacology were established in universities throughout the world. In the 20th century, and particularly in the years since World War II, pharmacological research has developed a vast array of new drugs, including antibiotics, such as penicillin, and many hormonal drugs, such as insulin and cortisone. Pharmacology is presently involved in the development of more effective versions of these and a vast array of other drugs through chemical synthesis in the laboratory. Pharmacology also seeks more efficient and effective ways of administering drugs through clinical research on large numbers of patients.

During the early 20th century, pharmacologists became aware that a relation exists between the chemical structure of a compound and the effects it produces in the body. Since that time, increasing emphasis has been placed on this aspect of pharmacology, and studies routinely describe the changes in drug action resulting from small changes in the chemical structure of the drug. Because most medical compounds are organic chemicals, pharmacologists who engage in such studies must necessarily have an understanding of organic chemistry.

Important basic pharmacological research is carried out in the research laboratories of pharmaceutical and chemical companies. After 1930 this area of pharmacological research underwent a vast and rapid expansion, particularly in the United States and Europe.

The work of pharmacologists in industry deals also with the exhaustive tests that must be made before promising new drugs can be introduced into medical use. Detailed observations of a drug's effects on all systems and organs of laboratory animals are necessary before the physician can accurately predict both the effects of the drug on patients and their potential toxicity to humans in general. The pharmacologist does not himself test the effects of drugs in patients; this is done only after exhaustive tests on animals and is usually conducted by physicians to determine the clinical effectiveness of new drugs. Constant testing is also required for the routine control and standardization of drug products and their potency and purity.

performance, with the reduction in edema resulting from improved cardiovascular function. Nevertheless, the observations in Withering's monograph led to a more rational and scientifically based use of digitalis and eventually other drugs.

ISOLATION AND SYNTHESIS OF COMPOUNDS

In the 1800s many important compounds were isolated from plants for the first time. About 1804 the active ingredient morphine was isolated from opium. In 1820 quinine (malaria treatment) was isolated from cinchona bark and colchicine (gout treatment) from autumn crocus. In 1833 atropine (variety of uses) was purified from *Atropa belladonna*, and in 1860 cocaine (local anesthetic) was isolated from coca leaves. Isolation and purification of these medicinal compounds was of tremendous importance for several reasons. First, accurate doses of the drugs could be administered, something that had not been possible previously because the plants contained unknown and variable amounts of the active drug. Second, toxic effects due to impurities in the plant products could be eliminated if only the pure active ingredients were used. Finally, knowledge of the chemical structure of pure drugs enabled laboratory synthesis of many structurally related compounds and the development of valuable drugs.

THE HISTORY OF PHARMACEUTICALS

This rendering depicts men harvesting the bark of the cinchona tree, which is native to South America, for use in the treatment of malaria.

Pain relief has been an important goal of medicine development for millennia. Prior to the mid-19th century, surgeons took great pride in the speed with which they could complete a surgical procedure.

Faster surgery meant that the patient would undergo the excruciating pain for shorter periods of time. In 1842 ether was first employed as an anesthetic during surgery, and chloroform followed soon after in 1847. These agents revolutionized the practice of surgery. After their introduction, careful attention could be paid to prevention of tissue damage, and longer and more complex surgical procedures could be carried out more safely. Although both ether and chloroform were employed in anesthesia for more than a century, their current use is severely limited by their side effects; ether is very flammable and explosive and chloroform may cause severe liver toxicity in some patients. However, because pharmaceutical chemists knew the chemical structures of these two anesthetics, they were able to synthesize newer anesthetics, which have many chemical similarities with ether and chloroform but do not burn or cause liver toxicity.

DISCOVERY OF ANTISEPTICS AND VACCINES

Prior to the development of anesthesia, many patients succumbed to the pain and stress of surgery. Many other patients had their wounds become infected and died as a result of their infection. In 1865 the British surgeon and medical scientist Joseph Lister initiated the era of antiseptic surgery in England. While many of the innovations of the antiseptic era are procedural (use of gloves and other sterile procedures), Lister also introduced the use of phenol as an anti-infective agent.

In the prevention of infectious diseases, an even more important innovation took place near the beginning of the 19th century with the introduction of smallpox vaccine. In the late 1790s the English surgeon Edward Jenner observed that milkmaids who had been infected with the relatively benign cowpox virus were protected against the much more deadly smallpox. After this observation he developed an immunization procedure based on the use of crude material from the cowpox lesions. This success was followed in 1885 by the development of rabies vaccine by the French chemist and microbiologist Louis Pasteur. Widespread vaccination programs have dramatically reduced the incidence of many infectious diseases that once were common. Indeed, vaccination programs have eliminated smallpox infections. The virus no longer exists in the wild, and, unless it is reintroduced from caches of smallpox virus held in laboratories in the United States and Russia, smallpox will no longer occur in humans. A similar effort is under way with widespread polio vaccinations; however, it remains unknown whether the vaccines will eliminate polio as a human disease.

EDWARD JENNER

At the age of 13, Edward Jenner (b. May 17, 1749, Berkeley, Gloucestershire, England—d. January 26, 1823, Berkeley) was apprenticed to a surgeon. In the following eight years Jenner acquired a sound knowledge of medical and surgical practice. On completing his apprenticeship at the age of 21, he went to London and became the house pupil of John Hunter, who was on the staff of St. George's Hospital and was one of the most prominent surgeons in London. After studying in London from 1770 to 1773, he returned to country practice in Berkeley and enjoyed substantial success.

Smallpox was widespread in the 18th century, and occasional outbreaks of special intensity resulted in a very high death rate. The only means of combating smallpox was a primitive form of vaccination called variolation—intentionally infecting a healthy person with the "matter" taken from a patient sick with a mild attack of the disease. The practice, which originated in China and India, was based on two distinct concepts: first, that one attack of smallpox effectively protected against any subsequent attack and, second, that a person deliberately infected with a mild case of the disease would safely acquire such protection. It was, in present-day terminology, an "elective" infection—i.e., one given to a person in good health. Unfortunately, the transmitted disease did not always remain mild, and mortality sometimes occurred. Furthermore, the inoculated person could disseminate the disease to others and thus act as a focus of infection.

Jenner had been impressed by the fact that a person who had suffered an attack of cowpox—a relatively harmless disease that

THE HISTORY OF PHARMACEUTICALS

could be contracted from cattle—could not take the smallpox—i.e., could not become infected whether by accidental or intentional exposure to smallpox. Pondering this phenomenon, Jenner concluded that cowpox not only protected against smallpox but could be transmitted from one person to another as a deliberate mechanism of protection.

In May 1796 Jenner found a young dairymaid, Sarah Nelmes, who had fresh cowpox lesions on her hand. On May 14, using matter from Sarah's lesions, he inoculated an eight-year-old boy, James Phipps, who had never had smallpox. Phipps became slightly ill over the course of the next 9 days but was well on the 10th. On July 1 Jenner inoculated the boy again, this time with smallpox matter. No disease developed; protection was complete. In 1798 Jenner, having added further

Edward Jenner vaccinates a child with the cowpox serum he developed to protect against smallpox.

(*continued on the next page*)

(*continued from the previous page*)

cases, published privately a slender book entitled *An Inquiry into the Causes and Effects of the Variolae Vaccinae*.

The reaction to the publication was not immediately favourable. Jenner went to London seeking volunteers for vaccination but, in a stay of three months, was not successful. In London vaccination became popularized through the activities of others, particularly the surgeon Henry Cline, to whom Jenner had given some of the inoculant, and the doctors George Pearson and William Woodville. Difficulties arose, some of them quite unpleasant; Pearson tried to take credit away from Jenner, and Woodville, a physician in a smallpox hospital, contaminated the cowpox matter with smallpox virus. Vaccination rapidly proved its value, however, and Jenner became intensely active in promoting it. The procedure spread rapidly to America and the rest of Europe and soon was carried around the world.

Despite errors and occasional chicanery, the death rate from smallpox plunged. Jenner received worldwide recognition and many honours, but he made no attempt to enrich himself through his discovery and actually devoted so much time to the cause of vaccination that his private practice and personal affairs suffered severely. Jenner not only received honours but also aroused opposition and found himself subjected to attacks and calumnies, despite which he continued his activities on behalf of vaccination. His wife, ill with tuberculosis, died in 1815, and Jenner retired from public life.

IMPROVEMENT IN DRUG ADMINISTRATION

While it may seem obvious today, it was not always clearly understood that medications must be delivered to the diseased tissue in order to be effective. Indeed, at times apothecaries made pills that were designed to be swallowed, pass through the gastrointestinal tract, be retrieved from the stool, and used again. While most drugs are effective and safe when taken orally, some are not reliably absorbed into the body from the gastrointestinal tract and must be delivered by other routes. In the middle of the 17th century, Richard Lower and Christopher Wren, working at the University of Oxford, demonstrated that drugs could be injected into the bloodstream of dogs using a hollow quill. In 1853 the French surgeon Charles Gabriel Pravaz invented the hollow hypodermic needle, which was first used in the treatment of disease in the same year by Scottish physician Alexander Wood. The hollow hypodermic needle had a tremendous influence on drug administration. Because drugs could be injected directly into the bloodstream, rapid and dependable drug action became more readily producible. Development of the hollow hypodermic needle also led to an understanding that drugs could be administered by multiple routes and was of great significance for the development of the modern science of pharmaceutics, or dosage form development.

NEW CLASSES OF PHARMACEUTICALS

In the latter part of the 19th century a number of important new classes of pharmaceuticals were developed. In 1869 chloral hydrate became the first synthetic sedative-hypnotic (sleep-producing) drug. In 1879 it was discovered that organic nitrates such as nitroglycerin could relax blood vessels, eventually leading to the use of these organic nitrates in the treatment of heart problems. In 1875 several salts of salicylic acid were developed for their antipyretic (fever-reducing) action. Salicylate-like preparations in the form of willow bark extracts (which contain salicin) had been in use for at least 100 years prior to the identification and synthesis of the purified compounds. In 1879 the artificial sweetener saccharin was introduced. In 1886 acetanilide, the first analgesic-antipyretic drug (relieving pain and fever), was introduced, but later, in 1887, it was replaced by the less toxic phenacetin. In 1899 aspirin (acetylsalicylic acid) became the most effective and popular anti-inflammatory, analgesic-antipyretic drug for at least the next 60 years. Cocaine, derived from the coca leaf, was the only known local anesthetic until about 1900, when the synthetic compound benzocaine was introduced. Benzocaine was the first of many local anesthetics with similar chemical structures and led to the synthesis and introduction of a variety of compounds with more efficacy and less toxicity.

TRANSITIONS IN DRUG DISCOVERY

In the late 19th and early 20th centuries, a number of social, cultural, and technical changes of importance to pharmaceutical discovery, development, and manufacturing were taking place. One of the most important changes occurred when universities began to encourage their faculties to form a more coherent understanding of existing information. Some chemists developed new and improved ways to separate chemicals from minerals, plants, and animals, while others developed ways to synthesize novel compounds. Biologists did research to improve understanding of the processes fundamental to life in species of microbes, plants, and animals. Developments in science were happening at a greatly accelerated rate, and the way in which pharmacists and physicians were educated changed. Prior to this transformation the primary means of educating physicians and pharmacists had been through apprenticeships. While apprenticeship teaching remained important to the education process (in the form of clerkships, internships, and residencies), pharmacy and medical schools began to create science departments and hire faculty to teach students the new information in basic biology and chemistry. New faculty were expected to carry out research or scholarship of their own. With the rapid advances in chemical separations and synthesis, single pharmacists did not have the skills and resources to make the newer, chemically pure drugs. Instead, large chemical and pharmaceutical companies began to appear and employed university-trained scientists equipped with knowledge of the latest technologies and information in their fields.

As the 20th century progressed, the benefits of medical, chemical, and biological research began to be appreciated by the general public and by politicians, prompting governments to develop mechanisms to provide support for university research. In the United States, for instance, the National Institutes of Health, the National Science Foundation, the Department of Agriculture, and many other agencies undertook their own research or supported research and discovery at universities that could then be used for pharmaceutical development. Nonprofit organizations were also developed to support research, including the Australian Heart Foundation, the American Heart Association, the Heart and Stroke Foundation of Canada, and H.E.A.R.T UK. The symbiotic relationship between large public institutions carrying out fundamental research and private companies making use of the new knowledge to develop and produce new pharmaceutical products has contributed greatly to the advancement of medicine.

EARLY EFFORTS IN THE DEVELOPMENT OF ANTI-INFECTIVE DRUGS

For much of history, infectious diseases were the leading cause of death in most of the world. The widespread use of vaccines and implementation of public health measures, such as building reliable sewer systems and chlorinating water to assure safe supplies for drinking, were of great benefit in decreasing the impact of infectious diseases in the industrialized world. However, even with these measures, pharmaceutical treatments for infectious diseases were needed. The first of these was arsphenamine, which was developed in 1910 by the German medical scientist Paul Ehrlich for the treatment of syphilis. Arsphenamine was the 606th chemical studied by Ehrlich in his quest for an antisyphilitic drug. Its efficacy was first demonstrated in mice with syphilis and then in humans. Arsphenamine was marketed with the trade name of Salvarsan and was used to treat syphilis until the 1940s, when it was replaced by penicillin. Ehrlich referred to his invention as chemotherapy, which is the use of a specific chemical to combat a specific infectious organism. Arsphenamine was important not only because it was the first synthetic compound to kill a specific invading microorganism

BIOPHARMACEUTICALS

but also because of the approach Ehrlich used to find it. In essence, he synthesized a large number of compounds and screened each one to find a chemical that would be effective. Screening for efficacy became one of the most important means used by the pharmaceutical industry to develop new drugs.

The next great advance in the development of drugs for treatment of infections came in the 1930s, when it was shown that certain azo dyes, which contained sulfonamide groups, were effective in treating streptococcal infections in mice. One of the dyes, known as Prontosil, was later found to be metabolized in the patient to sulfanilamide, which was the active antibacterial molecule. In 1933 Prontosil was given to the first patient, an infant with a systemic staphylococcal infection. The infant underwent a dramatic cure. In subsequent years many derivatives of sulfonamides, or sulfa drugs, were synthesized and tested for antibacterial and other activities.

DISCOVERY OF PENICILLIN

The first description of penicillin was published in 1929 by the Scottish bacteriologist Alexander Fleming. Fleming had been studying staphylococcal bacteria in the laboratory at St. Mary's Hospital in London. He noticed that a mold had contaminated one of his cultures, causing the bacteria in its vicinity to undergo lysis (membrane rupture) and die. Since the mold was from

Sir Alexander Fleming, pictured here in a lab, started an antibiotic revolution after his discovery of penicillin in 1928 and earned a Nobel Prize for his work in 1945.

the genus *Penicillium*, Fleming named the active antibacterial substance penicillin. At first the significance of Fleming's discovery was not widely recognized. It was more than 10 years later before British biochemist Ernst Boris Chain and Australian pathologist Howard Florey, working at the University of Oxford, showed that a crude penicillin preparation produced a dramatic curative effect when administered to mice with streptococcal infections.

The production of large quantities of penicillin was difficult with the facilities available to the investigators. However, by 1941 they had enough penicillin to carry out a clinical trial in several patients with severe staphylococcal and streptococcal infections. The effects of penicillin were remarkable, although there was not enough drug available to save the lives of all the patients in the trial.

In an effort to develop large quantities of penicillin, the collaboration of scientists at the United States Department of Agriculture's Northern Regional Research Laboratories in Peoria, Ill., was enlisted. The laboratories in Peoria had large fermentation vats that could be used in an attempt to grow an abundance of the mold. In England the first penicillin had been produced by growing the *Penicillium notatum* mold in small containers. However, *P. notatum* would not grow well in the large fermentation vats available in Peoria, so scientists from the laboratories searched for another strain of *Penicillium*. Eventually a strain of *Penicillium chrysogenum* that had been isolated from an overripe cantaloupe was found to grow very well in the deep culture vats. After the process of growing the penicillin-producing organisms was developed, pharmaceutical firms were recruited to further develop and market the drug for clinical use. The use of penicillin very quickly revolutionized the treatment of serious bacterial infections. The discovery, development, and marketing of penicillin provides an excellent example of the beneficial collaborative interaction of not-for-profit researchers and the pharmaceutical industry.

ISOLATION OF INSULIN

The vast majority of hormones were identified, had their biological activity defined, and were synthesized in the first half of the 20th century. Illnesses relating to their excess or deficiency were also beginning to be understood at that time. Hormones, produced in specific organs, released into the circulation, and carried to other organs, significantly affect metabolism and homeostasis. Some examples of hormones are insulin (from the pancreas), epinephrine (or adrenaline; from the adrenal medulla), thyroxine (from the thyroid gland), cortisol (from the adrenal cortex), estrogen (from the ovaries), and testosterone (from the testes). As a result of discovering these hormones and their mechanisms of action in the body, it became possible to treat illnesses of deficiency or excess effectively. The discovery and use of insulin to treat diabetes is an example of these developments.

In 1869 Paul Langerhans, a medical student in Germany, was studying the histology of the pancreas. He noted that this organ has two distinct types of cells—acinar cells, now known to secrete digestive enzymes, and islet cells (now called islets of Langerhans). The function of islet cells was suggested in 1889 when German physiologist and pathologist Oskar Minkowski and German physician Joseph von Mering showed that removing the pancreas from a dog caused the animal to exhibit a disorder quite similar to human diabetes mellitus (elevated blood glucose and metabolic changes). After this discovery, a number of scientists in various parts of the world attempted to extract the active substance from the pancreas so that it could be used to treat diabetes. We now know that these attempts were largely unsuccessful because the digestive enzymes present in the acinar cells metabolized the insulin from the islet cells when the pancreas was disrupted.

One of the first successful attempts to isolate the active substance was reported in 1921 by Romanian physiologist Nicolas C. Paulescu, who discovered a substance called pancrein in pancreatic extracts from dogs. Paulescu found that diabetic dogs given an injection of pancrein experienced a temporary decrease in blood glucose levels. Although he did not purify pancrein, it is thought that the substance was insulin. That same year, working independently, Frederick Banting, a young Canadian surgeon in Toronto, persuaded a physiology professor to allow him use of a laboratory to search for the active substance from the pancreas. Banting guessed correctly that the islet cells secreted insulin, which was destroyed by enzymes from the acinar cells. By this time Banting had enlisted the support of Charles H. Best, a fourth-year medical student. Together they tied off the pancreatic ducts through which acinar cells release the digestive enzymes. This insult caused the acinar cells to die. Subsequently, the remainder of the pancreas was homogenized and

An illustration of Canadian scientists Frederick G. Banting and Charles H. Best in the laboratory, testing insulin on a diabetic dog, August 14, 1921.

extracted with ethyl alcohol and acid. The extract thus obtained decreased blood glucose levels in dogs with a form of diabetes. Banting and Best worked with Canadian chemist James B. Collip and Scottish physiologist J.J.R. Macleod to obtain purified insulin, and shortly thereafter, in 1922, a 14-year-old boy with severe diabetes was the first human to be treated successfully with the pancreatic extracts.

After this success other scientists became involved in the quest to develop large quantities of purified insulin extracts. Eventually, extracts from pig and cow pancreases created a sufficient and reliable supply of insulin. For the next 50 years most of the insulin used to treat diabetes was extracted from porcine and bovine sources. There are only slight differences in chemical structure between bovine, porcine, and human insulin, and their hormonal activities are essentially equivalent. Today, as a result of recombinant DNA technology, most of the insulin used in therapy is synthesized by pharmaceutical companies and is identical to human insulin.

IDENTIFICATION OF VITAMINS

Vitamins are organic compounds that are necessary for body metabolism and, generally, must be provided from the diet. For centuries many diseases of dietary deficiency had been recognized, although not well defined. Most of the vitamin deficiency disorders were biochemically and physiologically defined in the late 19th and early 20th centuries. The discovery of thiamin (vitamin B1) exemplifies how vitamin deficiencies and their treatment were discovered.

Thiamin deficiency produces beriberi, a word from the Sinhalese meaning "extreme weakness." The symptoms include spasms and rigidity of the legs, possible paralysis of a limb, personality disturbances, and depression. This disease became widespread in Asia in the 19th century because steam-powered rice mills produced polished rice, which lacked the vitamin-rich husk. A dietary deficiency was first suggested as the cause of beriberi in 1880 when a new diet was instituted for the Japanese navy. When fish, meat, barley, and vegetables were added to the sailor's diet of polished rice, the incidence of beriberi in the navy was significantly reduced. In 1897 the Dutch physician Christiaan Eijkman was working in Java when he showed that fowl fed a diet of polished rice developed symptoms similar to beriberi. He was also able to demonstrate that unpolished rice in the diet prevented and cured the symptoms in fowl and humans. By 1912 a highly concentrated extract of the active ingredient was prepared by the Polish biochemist Casimir Funk, who recognized that it belonged to a new class of essential foods called vitamins. Thiamin was isolated in 1926 and its chemical structure determined in 1936. The chemical structures of the other vitamins were determined prior to 1940.

EMERGENCE OF MODERN DISEASES AND TREATMENT

The rapid decline in the number of deaths from infections due to the development of vaccines and antibiotics led to the unveiling of a new list of deadly diseases in the industrialized world during the second half of the 20th century. Included in this list are cardiovascular disease, cancer, and stroke. While these remain the three leading causes of death today, a great deal of progress in decreasing mortality and disability caused by these diseases has been made since the 1940s. As with treatment of any complex disease, there are many events of importance in the development of effective therapy. For decreasing death and disability from cardiovascular diseases and stroke, one of the most important developments was the discovery of effective treatments for hypertension (high blood pressure)—i.e., the discovery of thiazide diuretics. For decreasing death and disability from cancer, one very important step was the development of cancer chemotherapy.

HYPERTENSION

Hypertension has been labeled the silent killer. It usually

has minimal or no symptoms and typically is not regarded as a primary cause of death. Untreated hypertension increases the incidence and severity of cardiovascular diseases and stroke. Before 1950 there were no effective treatments for hypertension. U.S. Pres. Franklin D. Roosevelt died after a stroke in 1945, despite a large effort by his physicians to control his very high blood pressure by prescribing sedatives and rest.

When sulfanilamide was introduced into therapy, one of the side effects it produced was metabolic acidosis (acid-base imbalance). After further study, it was learned that the acidosis was caused by inhibition of the enzyme carbonic anhydrase. Inhibition of carbonic anhydrase produces diuresis (urine formation). Subsequently, many sulfanilamide-like compounds were synthesized and screened for their ability to inhibit carbonic anhydrase. Acetazolamide, which was developed by scientists at Lederle Laboratories (now a part of Wyeth Pharmaceuticals, Inc.), became the first of a class of diuretics that serve as carbonic anhydrase inhibitors. In an attempt to produce a carbonic anhydrase inhibitor more effective than acetazolamide, chlorothiazide was synthesized by a team of scientists led by Dr. Karl Henry Beyer at Merck & Co., Inc., and became the first successful thiazide diuretic. While acetazolamide causes diuresis by increasing sodium bicarbonate excretion, chlorothiazide was found to increase sodium chloride excretion. More importantly, by the mid-1950s it had been shown that chlorothiazide lowers blood pressure in patients with hypertension. Over the next 50 years many other classes of drugs that lower blood pressure (antihypertensive drugs) were added to the physician's armamentarium for treatment of hypertension. Partially as a result of effective treatment of this disease, the death rate from cardiovascular diseases and stroke decreased dramatically during this period.

The discovery of chlorothiazide exemplifies two important pathways to effective drug development. The first is screening for a biological effect. Thousands of drugs have been developed through effective screening for a biological activity. The second pathway is serendipity—i.e., making fortunate discoveries by chance. While creating experiments that can lead to chance outcomes does not require particular scientific skill, recognizing the importance of accidental discoveries is one of the hallmarks of sound science. Many authorities doubt that Fleming was the first scientist to notice that when agar plates were contaminated with *Penicillium* mold, bacteria did not grow near the mold. However, what made Fleming great was that he was the first to recognize the importance of what he had seen. In the case of chlorothiazide, it was serendipitous that sulfanilamide was found to cause metabolic acidosis, and it was serendipitous that chlorothiazide was recognized to cause sodium chloride excretion and an antihypertensive effect.

EARLY PROGRESS IN CANCER DRUG DEVELOPMENT

Sulfur mustard was synthesized in 1854. By the late 1880s it was recognized that sulfur mustard could cause blistering of the skin, eye irritation possibly leading to blindness, and severe lung injury if inhaled. In 1917 during World War I, sulfur mustard was first used as a chemical weapon. By 1919 it was realized that exposure to sulfur mustard also produced very serious systemic toxicities. Among other effects, it caused leukopenia (decreased white blood cells) and damage to bone marrow and lymphoid tissue. During the interval between World War I and World War II there was extensive research into the biological and chemical effects of nitrogen mustards (chemical analogs of sulfur mustard) and similar chemical-warfare compounds. The toxicity of nitrogen mustard on lymphoid tissue caused researchers to study the effect of nitrogen mustard on lymphomas in mice. In the early 1940s nitrogen mustard (mechlorethamine) was discovered to be effective in the treatment of human lymphomas. The efficacy of this treatment led to the widespread realization that chemotherapy for cancer could be effective. In turn, this realization led to extensive research, discovery, and development of other cancer chemotherapeutic agents.

THE PHARMACEUTICAL INDUSTRY IN THE MODERN ERA

The pharmaceutical industry has become a large and very complex enterprise. At the end of the 20th century, most of the world's largest pharmaceutical companies were located in North America, Europe, and Japan; many of the largest were multinational, having research, manufacturing, and sales taking place in multiple countries. Since pharmaceuticals can be quite profitable, many countries are trying to develop the infrastructure necessary for drug companies in their countries to become larger and to compete on a worldwide scale. The industry has also come to be characterized by outsourcing. That is, many companies contract with specialty manufacturers or research firms to carry out parts of the drug development process for them. Others try to retain most of the processes within their own company. Since the pharmaceutical industry is driven largely by profits and competition—each company striving to be the first to find cures for specific diseases—it is anticipated that the industry will continue to change and evolve over time.

EMERGENCE OF THE BIOPHARMACEUTICAL INDUSTRY

Although biopharmaceuticals—in the sense of drugs

THE HISTORY OF PHARMACEUTICALS

derived from living organisms—have been around about as long as pharmaceuticals of any kind, the modern biopharmaceutical industry was really born with the development of genetic engineering.

Once James Watson and Francis Crick discovered the double-helix model of DNA in 1953, researchers began working on and with human, animal and plant genetic material in a whole new way. As more and more was learned about the structure and actions of DNA, scientists begin to discover new ways to modify it. With the possibility of directly manipulating DNA, changes in the genetic makeup of a species that once could only have been achieved through decades of selective breeding might instead be accomplished within months. That promise was achieved with the development of recombinant DNA technology.

RECOMBINANT DNA TECHNOLOGY

Recombinant DNA (rDNA) technology is the recombining of DNA molecules from two different species that are inserted into a host organism to produce new genetic combinations that are of value to science, medicine, agriculture, or industry.

Recombinant DNA technology enables scientists to isolate a gene, determine its nucleotide sequence, study its transcripts, mutate it in highly specific ways, and reinsert the modified sequence into a living organism. The processes of DNA cloning and sequencing are used to compare different organisms for evolutionary relatedness and to determine gene function. Recombinant DNA technology can also be used to study mutations and their biological effects, such as the role of specific mutations in disease or abnormal drug response.

The technology was largely the work of Paul Berg, Herbert W. Boyer, and Stanley N. Cohen. In 1971, Berg, working at Stanford University, successfully spliced a bit of the DNA of a bacterial virus known as lambda into the DNA of simian virus SV40, producing the first man-made recombinant DNA. This achievement was highlighted in the award ceremony at which he received the 1980 Nobel Prize in Chemistry, jointly with Walter Gilbert and Frederick Sanger.

Berg did not immediately take the next logical step—introducing rDNA into another organism—because of public worry over the potential dangers. Berg, who was chair of the National Academy of Science's Committee on Recombinant DNA Molecules, played an active role in the public and scientific debate, which led to the issuing of guidelines by the National Institutes of Health for the safe conduct of rDNA research. With additional research and examination, the guidelines were adjusted to reflect the reality that the risks were less than originally thought.

However, that next step of inserting rDNA into another organism *was* taken in short order by Herbert Boyer at the University of California at San Francisco,

THE HISTORY OF PHARMACEUTICALS

in collaboration with Stanley Cohen of Stanford. They inserted rDNA into bacteria in such a way that the foreign DNA would replicate naturally. In the spring of 1973 they successfully introduced resistance to the antibiotic tetracycline into *Escherichia coli* bacteria through rDNA technology. They moved on to more complex experiments, including one that proved it was possible to transfer genetic material between species (successfully propagating DNA from *Staphylococcus*, another species of bacteria, and more significantly from the South African clawed frog, in *E. coli*.)

GENENTECH LEADS THE WAY

The achievements of Boyer and Cohen demonstrated that it should be feasible to incorporate human genetic information into bacteria. Commercialization still seemed a long way off: potential investors did not think the technology was advanced enough to spend money on yet, and scientists feared trying to make money off of the technology too early might endanger basic research.

For that reason, when Boyer agreed to a meeting in April 1976 with a young venture capitalist named Robert Swanson, he scheduled only ten minutes for it. But three hours later, Boyer and Swanson had come up with the idea for Genentech, which would become the world's first successful biotech company. Many other start-ups would follow in short order, but Genentech hit the ground running. Just a year later, in the fall of 1977, Boyer at UCSF and Keiichi Itakura at the City of Hope Medical Center in Duarte, California, modified bacteria to produce the mammalian protein somatostatin, which is produced in the human brain and plays a major role in regulating the growth hormone. The recombinant somatostatin was shown to be virtually identical to that produced in humans.

Then, in 1978, Boyer and Itakura constructed a plasmid that coded for human insulin.

INSULIN: THE FIRST RDNA BIOPHARMACEUTICAL

Diabetics who are unable to produce enough insulin in their bodies receive regular injections of the hormone, which are often customized according to their individual and variable requirements.

Human insulin is a small protein composed of 51 amino acids and has a molecular weight of 5,808 daltons. The amino acid sequence and chemical structure of insulin had been known for a number of years: the synthesis of sheep insulin had been reported in 1963 and human insulin in 1966. What was lacking was a synthetic process capable of producing the quantities necessary to supply market needs. Boyer and Itakura's success in getting *E. coli* to produce human insulin provided that process.

Until the development of rDNA-produced human insulin, insulin was isolated from the pancreases of slaughtered animals. The process was both complex and expensive. It took insulin from as

THE HISTORY OF PHARMACEUTICALS

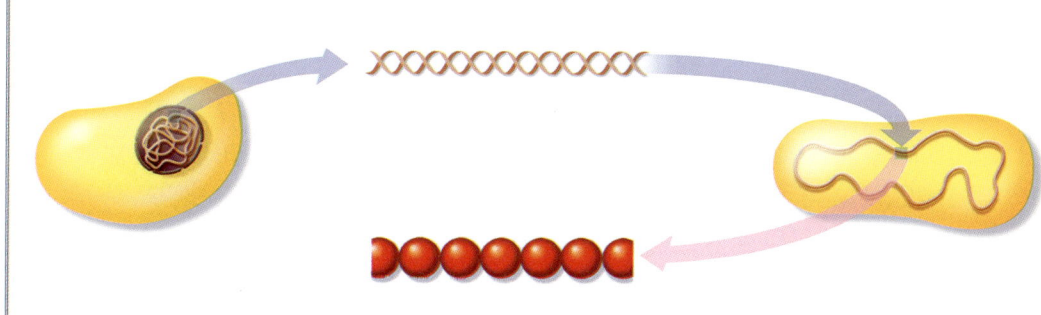

Plasmids with part of the gene for human insulin production (left) are extracted and inserted into the genome of bacteria (right). The final stage in the process is the production of human insulin.

many as 100 pig pancreases per diabetic patient per year to meet the need. And although the hormone obtained from pigs (and also cattle) differed only slightly from the human version, some patients did develop dangerous allergic reactions to it.

In the Genentech technique, small rings of DNA called plasmids, each containing part of the gene for the production of human insulin, were inserted into strains of *E. coli*, which then produced one or the other of the two insulin chains. These were then isolated separately before being combined and converted with enzymes into active insulin.

Eli Lilly and Company signed a joint-venture agreement with Genentech to develop the production process for the new rDNA insulin, called Humulin. In 1982 Humulin was approved by the FDA, and became the first rDNA-produced biopharmaceutical to

TREATING DIABETES

Human insulin may be given as a form that is identical to the natural form found in the body, which acts quickly but transiently, or as a form that has been biochemically modified so as to prolong its action for up to 24 hours.

The optimal regimen is one that most closely mimics the normal pattern of insulin secretion, which is a constant low level of insulin secretion plus a pulse of secretion after each meal. This can be achieved by administration of a long-acting insulin preparation once daily plus administration of a rapid-acting insulin preparation with or just before each meal. Patients also have the option of using an insulin pump, which allows them to control variations in the rate of insulin administration. A satisfactory compromise for some patients is twice-daily administration of mixtures of intermediate-acting and short-acting insulin.

Patients taking insulin also may need to vary food intake from meal to meal, according to their level of activity; as exercise frequency and intensity increase, less insulin and more food intake may be necessary.

The use of rDNA technology in the production of human insulin has eliminated dependence on animal pancreases and helped more than 200 million diabetics around the world.

Research into other areas of insulin therapy include pancreas transplantation, beta cell transplantation, implantable mechanical insulin infusion systems, and the generation of beta cells from existing exocrine cells in the pancreas. Patients with type I diabetes have been treated by transplantation of the pancreas or of the islets of Langerhans. However, limited quantities of pancreatic tissue are available for transplantation, prolonged immunosuppressive therapy is needed, and there is a high likelihood that the transplanted tissue will be rejected even when the patient is receiving immunosuppressive therapy. Attempts to improve the outcome of transplantation and to develop mechanical islets are ongoing.

appear on the market.

By virtue of being the first to be approved, synthesized human insulin often receives the spotlight in any discussion of the history of the modern biopharmaceutical industry. However, in some ways, the production of human growth hormone by recombinant DNA technology, first approved for use in 1985, was more important.

Prior to the availability of human insulin, most people with diabetes could at least be treated with the bovine or porcine insulin products, which had been available for 50 years. Unlike insulin, the effects imparted by growth hormone are different for every species. Therefore, prior to the synthesis of human growth hormone, the only source of the human hormone was from cadaver pituitaries. There are now a number of recombinant preparations of human growth hormone and other human peptides and proteins on the market.

GROWTH AND CONSOLIDATION

Hoping to match Genentech's amazing success, thousands of new biotechnology companies sprang up all over the world during the 1990s. Many were offshoots of private research institutes, formed by scientists hoping to make money from their discoveries. The biotech industry joined with the information technology industry to fuel the stock market boom at the end of the decade. Some of that investor exuberance was misplaced, and many of the startups eventually failed. However, the investment was crucial to getting the startups that *did* survive off the ground.

Developing any new drug up to the point it can be approved for sale is not only lengthy but risky and hugely expensive, mainly because of the high number of drugs that fail. In traditional drug synthesis, only one of every 100,000 to 200,000 chemically synthesized molecules becomes an approved drug in the pharmacy. The manufactured complex molecules of biopharmaceutical medicines have a better chance of making it to market, but they are also much more difficult and expensive to produce than drugs made through simple chemical synthesis.

As a result, the original Genentech model of a small biotech company joining forces with a large, well-established pharmaceutical company is the norm today. Such mergers have brought greater stability and growth to the industry.

CHAPTER 2

DRUG DISCOVERY AND DEVELOPMENT

A variety of approaches are employed to identify chemical compounds that may be developed and marketed. The current state of the chemical and biological sciences required for pharmaceutical development dictates that 5,000 to 10,000 chemical compounds must undergo laboratory screening for each new drug approved for use in humans. Of the 5,000 to 10,000 com-

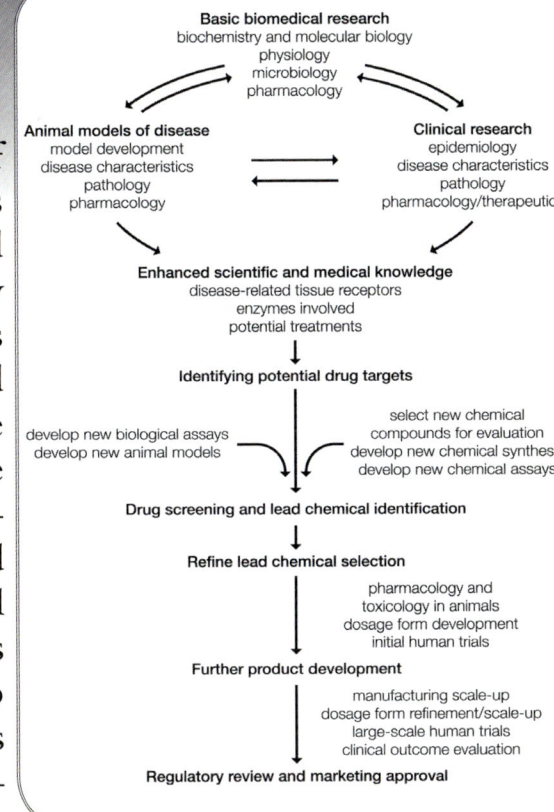

Flowchart of research and discovery processes used for drug development. These are the essential steps followed in the development of both synthetic drugs and biopharmaceuticals.

pounds that are screened, approximately 250 will enter preclinical testing, and 5 will enter clinical testing. The overall process from discovery to marketing of a drug can take 10 to 15 years.

RESEARCH AND DISCOVERY

Pharmaceuticals are produced as a result of activities carried out by a complex array of public and private organizations that are engaged in the development and manufacture of drugs. As part of this process, scientists at many publicly funded institutions carry out basic research in subjects such as chemistry, biochemistry, physiology, microbiology, and pharmacology. Basic research is almost always directed at developing new understanding of natural substances or physiological processes rather than being directed specifically at development of a product or invention. This enables scientists at public institutions and in private industry to apply new knowledge to the development of new products. The first steps in this process are carried out largely by basic scientists and physicians working in a variety of research institutions and universities. The results of their studies are published in scientific and medical journals. These results facilitate the identification of potential new targets for drug discovery. The targets could be a drug receptor, an enzyme, a biological transport process, or any other process involved in body metabolism. Once a target is identified, the bulk of the remaining work involved in discovery and development of a drug is carried out or directed by pharmaceutical companies.

CONTRIBUTION OF SCIENTIFIC KNOWLEDGE TO DRUG DISCOVERY

Two classes of antihypertensive drugs serve as an example of how enhanced biochemical and physiological knowledge of one body system contributed to drug development. Hypertension (high blood pressure) is a major risk factor for development of cardiovascular diseases. An important way to prevent cardiovascular diseases is to control high blood pressure. One of the physiological systems involved in blood pressure control is the renin-angiotensin system. Renin is an enzyme produced in the kidney. It acts on a blood protein to produce angiotensin. The details of the biochemistry and physiology of this system were worked out by biomedical scientists working at hospitals, universities, and government research laboratories around the world. Two important steps in production of the physiological effect of the renin-angiotensin system are the conversion of inactive angiotensin I to active angiotensin II by angiotensin-converting enzyme (ACE) and the interaction of angiotensin II with its physiologic receptors, including AT1 receptors. Angiotensin II interacts with AT1 receptors to raise blood pressure. Knowledge of the biochemistry and physiology of this system suggested to scientists that new drugs could be developed to lower abnormally high blood pressure.

A drug that inhibited ACE would decrease the formation of angiotensin II. Decreasing angiotensin II formation would, in turn, result in decreased activation of AT1 receptors. Thus, it was assumed that drugs that inhibit ACE would lower blood pressure. This assumption turned out to be correct, and a class of antihypertensive drugs called ACE inhibitors was developed. Similarly, once the role of AT1 receptors in blood pressure maintenance was understood, it was assumed that drugs that could block AT1 receptors would produce antihypertensive effects. Once again, this assumption proved correct, and a second class of antihypertensive drugs, the AT1 receptor antagonists, was developed. Agonists are drugs or naturally occurring substances that activate physiologic receptors, whereas antagonists are drugs that block those receptors. In this case, angiotensin II is an agonist at AT1 receptors, and the antihypertensive AT1 drugs are antagonists. Antihypertensives illustrate the value of discovering novel drug targets that are useful for large-scale screening tests to identify lead chemicals for drug development.

DRUG SCREENING

Screening chemical compounds for potential pharmacological effects is a very important process for drug discovery and development. Virtually every chemical and pharmaceutical company in the world has a library of chemical compounds that have been synthesized over many decades.

SOURCES OF COMPOUNDS

Historically, many diverse chemicals have been derived from natural products such as plants, animals, and microorganisms. Many more chemical compounds are available from university chemists. Additionally, automated, high-output, combinatorial chemistry methods have added hundreds of thousands of new compounds. Whether any of these millions of compounds have the characteristics that will allow them to become drugs remains to be discovered through rapid, high-efficiency drug screening.

LEAD CHEMICAL IDENTIFICATION

It took Paul Ehrlich years to screen the 606 chemicals that resulted in the development of arsphenamine as the first effective drug treatment for syphilis. From about the time of Ehrlich's success (1910) until the latter half of the 20th century, most screening tests for potential new drugs relied almost exclusively on screens in whole animals such as rats and mice. Ehrlich screened his compounds in mice with syphilis, and his procedures proved to be much more efficient than those of his contemporaries. Since the latter part of the 20th century, automated in vitro screening techniques have allowed tens of thousands of chemical compounds to be screened for efficacy in a single day. In large-capacity in vitro screens, individual chemicals

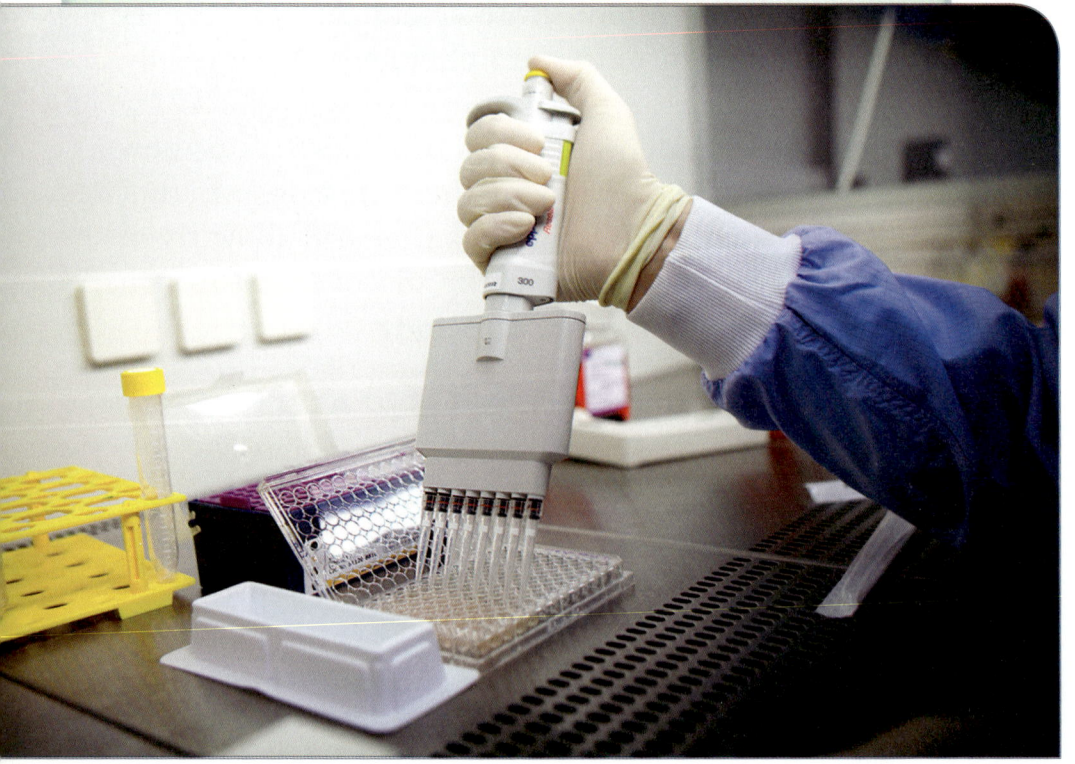

Microtiter plates, like the ones seen here, have helped scientists to more efficiently screen chemical compounds for their effectiveness on drug targets.

DRUG DISCOVERY AND DEVELOPMENT

are mixed with drug targets in small, test-tube-like wells of microtiter plates, and desirable interactions of the chemicals with the drug targets are identified by a variety of chemical techniques. The drug targets in the screens can be cell–free (enzyme, drug receptor, biological transporter, or ion channel), or they can contain cultured bacteria, yeasts, or mammalian cells. Chemicals that interact with drug targets in desirable ways become known as leads and are subjected to further developmental tests. Also, additional chemicals with slightly altered structures may be synthesized if the lead compound does not appear to be ideal. Once a lead chemical is identified, it will undergo several years of animal studies in pharmacology and toxicology to predict future human safety and efficacy.

LEAD COMPOUNDS FROM NATURAL PRODUCTS

Another very important way to find new drugs is to isolate chemicals from natural products. Digitalis, ephedrine, atropine, quinine, colchicine, and cocaine were purified from plants. Thyroid hormone, cortisol, and insulin originally were isolated from animals, whereas penicillin and other antibiotics were derived from microbes. In many cases plant-derived products were used for hundreds or thousands of years by indigenous peoples from around the world prior to their "discovery" by scientists from industrialized countries. In most cases these indigenous peoples

TAXOL AND THE PACIFIC YEW

As a member of the yew family (Taxaceae), the Pacific yew (*Taxus brevifolia*) has flat, evergreen needles and produces red, berrylike fruits. The toxicity of members of the yew family was described in ancient Greek literature. Indeed, the genus name *Taxus* derives from the Greek word *toxon*, which can be translated as toxin or poison. Pliny the Elder described people who died after drinking wine that had been stored in containers made from yew wood. Julius Caesar described how one of his enemies, Catuvolcus, poisoned himself using a yew plant. The early Japanese used yew plant parts to induce abortion and to treat diabetes, and Native Americans used yew to treat arthritis and fever. In part because of widespread historical accounts of the pronounced biological effects inherent in members of the yew family, samples of the Pacific yew were included in screens for potential anticancer drugs.

This screening process was initiated as a cooperative venture between the United States Department of Agriculture (USDA) and the National Cancer Institute (NCI) of the United States. Extracts from the Pacific yew were tested against two cancer cell lines in 1964 and found to have promising effects. After a sufficient quantity of the extract was prepared, the active compound, taxol, was isolated in 1969. In 1979 pharmacologist Susan Horwitz and her coworkers at Yeshiva University's Albert Einstein College of Medicine reported a unique mechanism of action for taxol. In 1983 NCI-supported clinical trials with taxol were begun, and by 1989 NCI-supported clinical researchers at Johns Hopkins University reported very positive effects in the treatment of ovarian cancer. Also in 1989 the NCI reached an agreement with Bristol-Myers Squibb to increase production, supplies, and marketing of taxol. Taxol marketing for the treatment of ovarian cancer began in 1992. Bristol-Myers Squibb applied to trademark the name taxol, which became Taxol®, and the generic name became paclitaxel.

Initially, the sole source of taxol was the bark of the Pacific yew, native to the old-growth forests along the northwest coast of

(*continued on the next page*)

A researcher collects bark from a Pacific yew for use in the development of the cancer treatment drug Taxol®. With the adoption of a semisynthetic process for producing taxol, damage to the plant and its ecosystem have decreased.

(*continued from the previous page*)

the United States and in British Columbia. This led to considerable public controversy. Environmental groups feared that harvesting of the yew would endanger its survival. It took the bark of between three and ten 100-year-old plants to make enough drug to treat one patient. There were also fears that harvesting the yew would lead to environmental damage to the area and could potentially destroy much of the habitat for the endangered spotted owl. After several years of controversy, Bristol-Myers Squibb adopted a semisynthetic process for making taxol. This process uses a precursor, which is chemically converted to taxol. The precursor is extracted from the needles (renewable biomass) of *Taxus baccata*, which is grown in the Himalayas and in Europe. Although there were some political controversies surrounding the discovery and development of taxol, the story of its development and marketing provides another example of how public and private enterprise can cooperate in the development of new discoveries and new drugs.

learned which plants had medicinal value the same way they learned which plants were safe to eat—trial and error. Ethnopharmacology is a branch of medical science in which the medicinal products used by isolated or primitive people are investigated using modern scientific techniques. In some cases chemicals with desirable pharmacological properties are isolated and eventually become drugs with properties recognizable in the natural product. In other cases chemicals with

DRUG DISCOVERY AND DEVELOPMENT

unique or unusual chemical structures are identified in the natural product. These new chemical structures are then subjected to drug screens to determine if they have potential pharmacological or medicinal value. There are many cases where such chemical structures and their synthetic analogs are developed as drugs with uses unlike those of the natural product. One such compound is the important anticancer drug taxol, which was isolated from the Pacific yew (*Taxus brevifolia*).

STRATEGIES FOR DRUG DESIGN AND PRODUCTION

There are various strategies for the design and production of new drugs, and they can vary depending on whether the drug is created using chemical synthesis or through a biopharmaceutical process.

Once a substance has been found to have a beneficial biological effect, researchers can build on that knowledge to create new drugs that may be more effective, less toxic, or otherwise improved. New technology, especially the development of computers and robotics, has drastically reduced the amount of time it takes to synthesize new compounds, which can then be examined for their medicinal value.

On the biopharmaceutical side, rDNA technology allows for the synthesizing of human proteins and other biologically derived molecules that would otherwise be difficult or impossible to obtain in sufficient quantities for use in medicine. And new techniques for matching drugs to individuals' specific genetic makeup are ushering in a revolutionary new era of personalized medicine, in which therapies will be designed and produced that are more finely targeted and more effective than ever before.

STRUCTURE-ACTIVITY RELATIONSHIP

The term *structure-activity relationship* (SAR) is now used to describe the process used by Ehrlich to develop arsphenamine, the first successful treatment for syphilis. In essence, Ehrlich synthesized a series of structurally related chemical compounds and tested each one to determine its pharmacological activity. In subsequent years many drugs were developed using the SAR approach. For example, the ß-adrenergic antagonists (antihypertensive drugs) and the ß2 agonists (asthma drugs) were developed initially by making minor modifications to the chemical structure of the naturally occurring agonists epinephrine (adrenaline) and norepinephrine (noradrenaline). Once a series of chemical compounds had been synthesized and tested, medicinal chemists began to understand which chemical substitutions would produce agonists and which would produce antagonists. Additionally, substitutions that would cause metabolic enzyme blockade and increase the gastrointestinal absorption or duration of action began to be understood. Three-dimensional molecular models

DRUG DISCOVERY AND DEVELOPMENT

of agonists and antagonists that fit the drug receptor allowed scientists to gain important information about the three-dimensional structure of the drug receptor site. By the 1960s SAR had been further refined by creating mathematical relationships between chemical structure and biological activity. This refinement, which became known as quantitative structure-activity relationship, simplified the search for chemical structures that could activate or block various drug receptors.

COMPUTER-AIDED DESIGN OF DRUGS

(Left) A cell reacts to an agonist drug (in green). (Right) A cell reacts to an antagonist drug. The pink represents a naturally occurring substance at the receptor site. Agonists activate physiologic receptors, and antagonists block them.

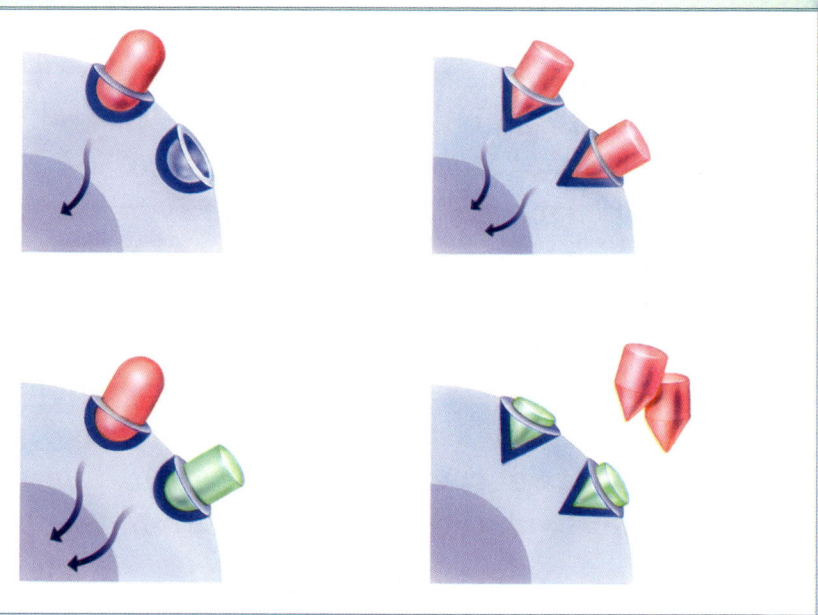

A further refinement of new drug design and production was provided by the process of computer-aided design (CAD). With the availability of powerful computers and sophisticated graphics software, it is possible for the medicinal chemist to design new molecules and evaluate their potential interaction with a receptor or an enzyme before they are synthesized. This means that the chemist may be able to synthesize and test only the most promising compounds, thus allowing potential new drugs to be synthesized more efficiently and cheaply.

COMBINATORIAL CHEMISTRY

Combinatorial chemistry was a development of the 1990s. It originated in the field of peptide chemistry but has since become an important tool of the medicinal chemist. Traditional organic synthesis is essentially a linear process with molecular building blocks being assembled in a series of individual steps. Part A of the new molecule is joined to part B to form part AB. After part AB is made, part C can be joined to it to make ABC. This step-wise construction is continued until the new molecule is complete. Using this approach, a medicinal chemist can, on average, synthesize about 25 new compounds per year. In combinatorial chemistry, one might start with five compounds (A_1–A_5). These five compounds would be reacted with building blocks

B_1–B_5 and building blocks C_1–C_5. These reactions take place in parallel rather than in series, so that A_1 would combine with B_1, B_2, B_3, B_4, and B_5. Each one of these combinations would also combine with each of the C_1–C_5 building blocks, so that 125 compounds would be synthesized. Using robotic synthesis and combinatorial chemistry, hundreds of thousands of compounds can be synthesized in much less time than would have been required to synthesize a few compounds in the past.

SYNTHETIC HUMAN PROTEINS

As described in more detail earlier, an important milestone for medical science and for the pharmaceutical industry occurred in 1982, when regulatory and marketing approval for Humulin®, human insulin, was granted in the United Kingdom and the United States. This marketing approval was an important advancement because it represented the first time a clinically important, synthetic human protein had been made into a pharmaceutical product, and it launched the biopharmaceutical industry. Again, the venture was successful because of cooperative efforts between physicians and scientists working in research institutions, universities, hospitals, and the pharmaceutical industry.

PERSONALIZED MEDICINE

BIOPHARMACEUTICALS

A growing component of the development of new biopharmaceuticals is personalized medicine, which has the potential to "revive" medicines in development that have not proven successful previously.

Some drugs, when tested, do not benefit a broad population but may work extremely well in a particular subpopulation. For example, a product for the treatment of gastric cancer that had disappointing results in its trials was found to provide significant

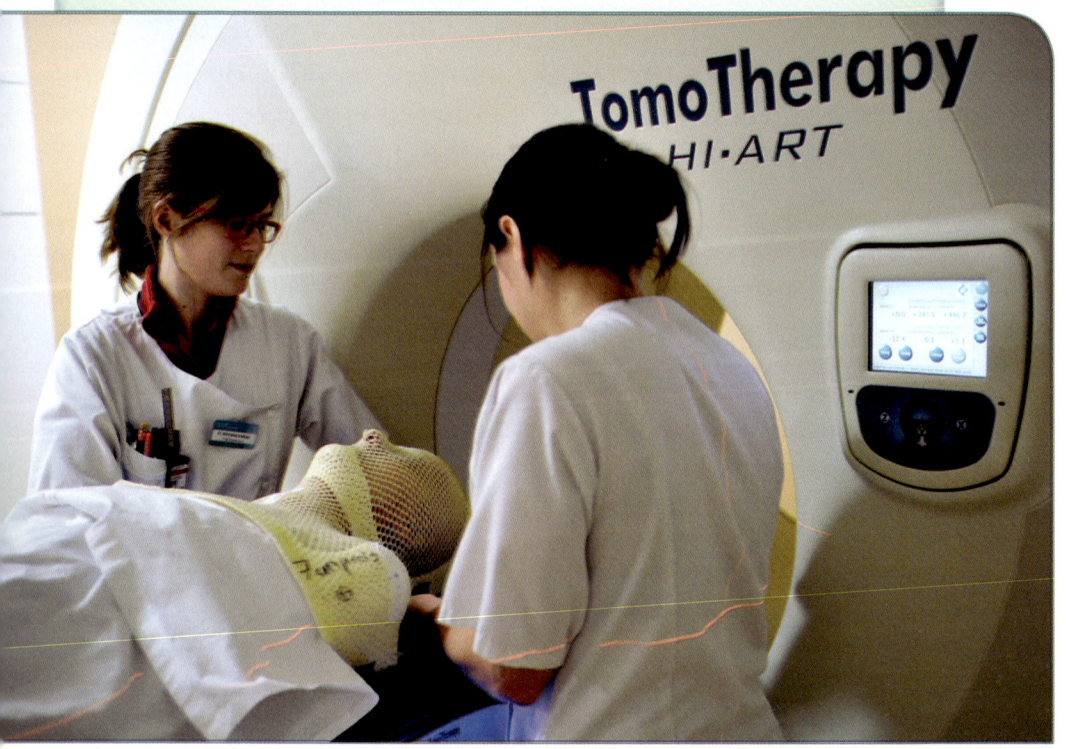

Personalized medicine has the potential to benefit cancer patients by introducing treatments tailored to work with their specific genetic makeup.

DRUG DISCOVERY AND DEVELOPMENT

benefit to a subset of patients whose gastric tumours expressed high levels of a protein involved in cell growth known as MET. The product blocked a protein that activates MET, which can contribute to cancer cell proliferation. The product almost doubled survival rates in that subset of patients.

Now the product is being studied as a possible treatment for other cancers in which MET plays a similar role, including prostate cancer, colorectal cancer, and small cell lung cancer.

Personalized medicine—the use of an individual's genetic makeup to inform diagnostic, preventative, or treatment decisions—is becoming increasingly common. The idea of tailored treatments has also become an important part of drug development, according to a 2010 survey by the Tufts Center for the Study of Drug Development.

CHAPTER 3
DRUG REGULATION AND APPROVAL

Concerns related to the efficacy and safety of drugs have caused most governments to develop regulatory agencies to oversee development and marketing of drug products and medical devices. Use of any drug carries with it some degree of risk of an adverse event. For most drugs the risk-to-benefit ratio is favourable; that is, the benefit derived from using the drug far outweighs the risk incurred from its use. However, there have been unfortunate circumstances in which drugs have caused considerable harm. The harm has come from drug products containing toxic impurities, from drugs with unrecognized severe adverse reactions, from adulterated drug products, and from fake or counterfeit drugs. Because of these issues, effective drug regulation is required to ensure the safety and efficacy of drugs for the general public.

PUBLIC INFLUENCE ON DRUG REGULATION

The process of drug regulation has evolved over time. Laws regulating drug marketing and development, government regulatory agencies with oversight of drug development and use, drug evaluation boards, drug information centres, and quality control laboratories have become part of the cooperative venture that produces and develops drugs. In some countries drug laws omit or exempt certain areas of pharmaceutical activity from regulation. For example, some countries exempt herbal or homeopathic products from regulation. In other countries there is very little regulation imposed on drug importation. Over time, the scope of drug laws and the authority vested in regulatory agencies have gradually expanded. In some instances, strengthening of drug laws has been the result of a drug-related catastrophe that prompted public demand for more restrictive legislation to provide more protection for the public. One such example occurred in the 1960s with thalidomide that was prescribed to treat morning sickness in pregnant women. Thalidomide had been on the market for several years before it was realized to be the causative agent of a rare birth defect, known as phocomelia, that had begun appearing at epidemic proportions. There was a dramatic reaction to the devastation caused by thalidomide, especially because it was considered a needless drug.

BIOPHARMACEUTICALS

Thalidomide caused many birth defects, such as the stunted arms of the child seen here, in West Germany and the United Kingdom during the late 1950s and early 1960s, resulting in stricter regulation of drugs.

At other times the public has perceived that drug regulation and regulatory authorities have been too restrictive or too cautious in approving drugs for the market. This concern typically has been related to individuals with serious or life-threatening illnesses who might benefit from drugs that have been denied market approval or whose approval has been inordinately delayed because regulations are too strict. At times, governments have responded to these concerns by streamlining drug laws and regulations. Examples of types of drugs given expedited approval are cancer drugs and AIDS drugs. Regulatory measures that make rapid approval of new drugs paramount sometimes have led to marketing of drugs with more toxicity than the public finds acceptable. Thus, drug regulations can and probably will remain in a state of flux, becoming more lax when the public perceives a need for new drugs and more strict following a drug catastrophe.

OBJECTIVES AND ORGANIZATION OF DRUG REGULATORY AGENCIES

Effective regulation of drugs requires a variety of functions. Important functions include (1) evaluation of safety and efficacy data from animal and clinical trials, (2) licensing and inspection of manufacturing facilities and distribution channels to assure that drugs are not contaminated, (3) monitoring of adverse drug reactions for investigational and marketed drugs, and (4) quality control of drug promotion and advertising to assure that safety and efficacy claims are accurate. In some countries all functions surrounding drug regulation come under a single agency. In others, particularly those with a federal system of government, some drug regulatory authority is assumed by state or provincial governments.

Around the world, financing of drug regulatory agencies varies. Many governments provide support for such agencies with revenue from general tax funds. The theory behind this type of financing is that the common good is served by effective regulations that provide for safe and effective medicines. In other countries the agencies are supported entirely by fees paid by the pharmaceutical firms seeking regulatory approval. In still other countries the work of drug regulatory agencies is supported by a mixture of direct government support and user fees. The World Health Organization (WHO) has developed international panels of experts in medicine, law, and pharmaceutical development that are responsible for recommending standards for national drug laws and regulations.

DRUG APPROVAL PROCESSES

Drug approval processes are designed to allow safe and effective drugs to be marketed. Drug regulatory agencies in various countries attempt to rely on premarketing scientific studies of the effects of drugs in animals and humans in order to determine if new drugs have a favourable risk-to-benefit ratio. Although most countries require similar types of premarketing studies to be completed, differences in specific regulations and guidelines exist. Thus,

DRUG REGULATION AND APPROVAL

if pharmaceutical firms wish to market their new drugs in many countries, they may face challenges created by the differing regulations and guidelines for premarketing studies. In order to simplify the approval process for multinational marketing of drugs, the WHO and many drug regulatory agencies have attempted to produce harmonization among regulations in various parts of the world. Harmonization, which aims to make regulations and guidelines more uniform, theoretically can decrease the cost of new drugs by decreasing the cost of development and regulatory approval. Because every new drug is somewhat different from preexisting ones, unforeseen safety or efficacy issues may arise during the regulatory review. Some of these issues may prompt an individual regulatory agency to require additional safety or efficacy studies. Thus, agreements on harmonization of regulations and guidelines can be more complicated and difficult to achieve than may seem to be the case.

The following sections describe in general terms the steps required for regulatory approval of drugs in one country—the United States. Although the descriptions are based on the Food and Drug Administration (FDA) regulations and guidelines, these requirements are similar to those in many other countries.

BIOPHARMACEUTICALS

FOOD AND DRUG ADMINISTRATION

The Food and Drug Administration (FDA) is an agency of the U.S. federal government authorized by Congress to inspect, test, approve, and set safety standards for foods and food additives, drugs, chemicals, cosmetics, and household and medical devices. First

In addition to overseeing a wide range of pharmaceutical research, the FDA must monitor food products and various devices. The FDA researcher here is monitoring the effects of electromagnetic interference on implantable medical devices.

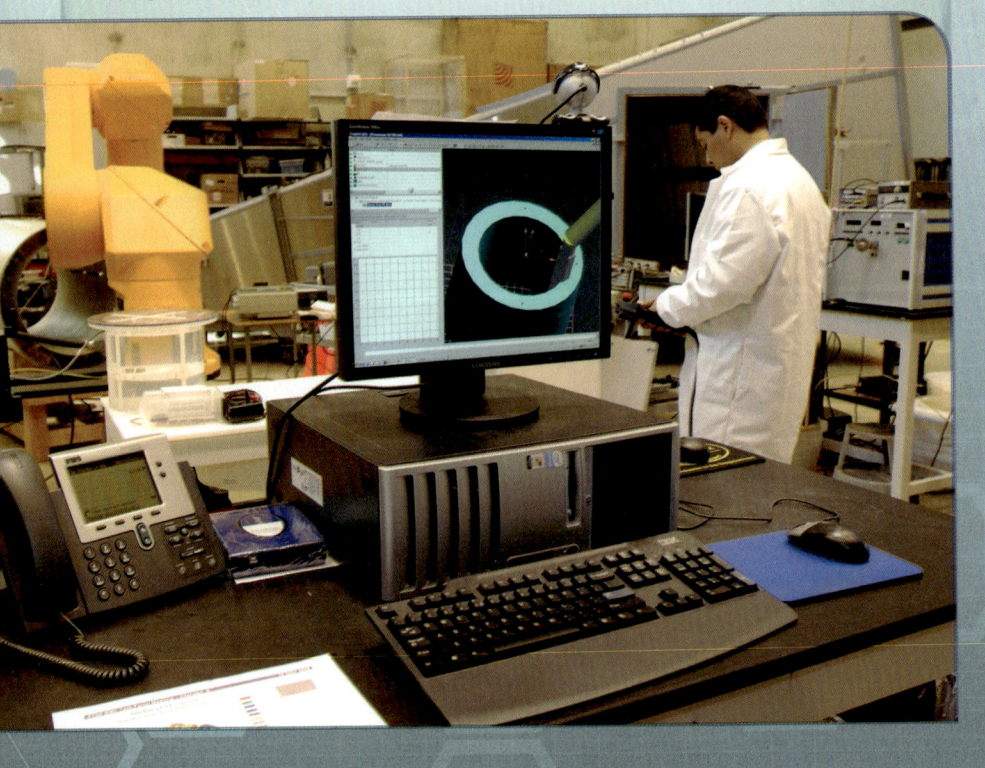

DRUG REGULATION AND APPROVAL

known as the Food, Drug, and Insecticide Administration when it was formed as a separate law enforcement agency in 1927, the FDA derives the greater part of its regulatory power from four laws: the Federal Food, Drug, and Cosmetic Act, which established safety and purity standards and provided for factory inspection and for legal remedy; the Fair Packaging and Labeling Act, which required honest, informative, and standardized labeling of products; the Radiation Control for Health and Safety Act, which was designed to protect consumers from possible excess radiation generated by X-ray machines, televisions, microwave ovens, and the like; and the Public Health Service Act, which gave the FDA authority over vaccines and serums and justified the agency's programs for milk sanitation and the inspection of restaurants and travel facilities.

Generally, the FDA is empowered to prevent untested products from being sold and to take legal action to halt sale of undoubtedly harmful products or of products which involve a health or safety risk. Through court procedure, the FDA can seize products and prosecute the persons or firms responsible for legal violation. FDA authority is limited to interstate commerce. The agency cannot control prices or directly regulate advertising except of prescription drugs and medical devices.

THE INVESTIGATIONAL NEW DRUG APPLICATION

Two important written documents are required from a pharmaceutical firm seeking regulatory approval from the FDA. The first is the Investigational New

Drug (IND) application. The IND is required for approval to begin studies of a new drug in humans. Clinical trials for new drugs are conducted prior to marketing as part of the development process. The purpose of these trials is to determine if newly developed drugs are safe and effective in humans. Pharmaceutical companies provide selected physicians with developmental drugs to be studied in their patients. These physicians recruit patients, provide them with the study drug, evaluate the effect of the drug on their disease, and record observations and clinical data.

There are three phases—designated Phase 1, Phase 2, and Phase 3—of human clinical studies required for drug approval and marketing. Phase 1 studies describe the first use of a new drug in humans. These studies are designed to determine the pharmacological and pharmacokinetic profile of the drug and to assess the adverse effects associated with increasing drug doses. Phase 1 studies provide important data to allow for the design of scientifically sound Phase 2 and Phase 3 studies. Phase 1 studies generally enroll 20–200 subjects who either are healthy or are patients with the disease that the drug is intended to treat. Phase 2 studies are designed primarily to assess the efficacy of the drug in the disease to be treated, although some data on adverse events or toxicities may also be collected. Phase 2 studies usually enroll several hundred patients. Phase 3 studies enroll several hundred to several thousand patients and are designed to collect data concerning both adverse

DRUG REGULATION AND APPROVAL

events and efficacy. When these data have been collected and analyzed, a judgment can be made about whether the drug should be marketed and if there should be specific restrictions on its use. An IND should contain information about the chemical makeup of the drug and the dosage form, summaries of animal pharmacology and toxicology studies, pharmacokinetic data, and information about any previous clinical investigations. Typically, Phase 1 protocols (descriptions of the trials to be conducted) are briefer and less detailed than Phase 2 and Phase 3 protocols.

Prior to its regulatory approval, a drug is generally restricted to use in patients who are formally enrolled in a clinical trial. In some cases a drug that has not yet been approved for marketing can be made available to patients with a life-threatening disease for whom no satisfactory

To conduct a clinical trial, researchers must first develop a study plan, or protocol, in which they describe the study's aims, the characteristics of the participants, the scientific approach, the outcome measures, and the plan for statistical evaluation of the data.

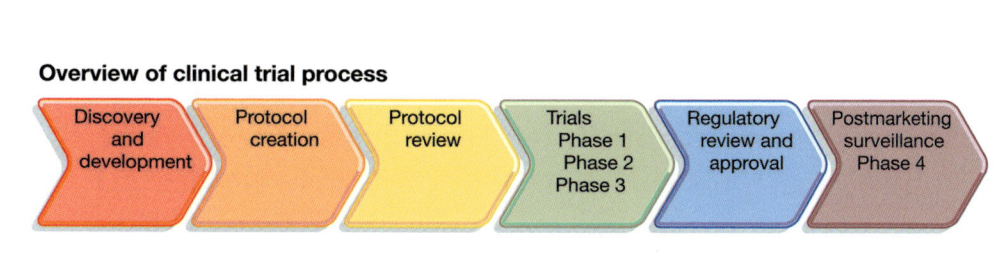

Overview of clinical trial process: Discovery and development → Protocol creation → Protocol review → Trials Phase 1 Phase 2 Phase 3 → Regulatory review and approval → Postmarketing surveillance Phase 4

alternative treatment is available. If the patient is not enrolled in one of the clinical trials, the drug can be made available under what is called a Treatment IND. A Treatment IND, which has sometimes been called a compassionate use protocol, is subject to regulatory requirements very similar to those of a regular IND.

THE NEW DRUG APPLICATION AND BIOLOGICS LICENSE APPLICATION

The second important regulatory document required by the FDA is either the New Drug Application (NDA) or the Biologics License Application (BLA). Both contain all of the information and data that the FDA requires for market approval of a drug. Depending on the intended use of the drug (one-time use or long-term use) and the risk associated with its intended use, INDs may be from tens to hundreds of pages long. In contrast, NDAs and BLAs typically are much larger and much more detailed. In some instances they can represent stacks of documents up to several metres high. Basically, an NDA or BLA is a detailed and comprehensive report on what is known about the new drug under review. It contains technical sections on (1) chemistry, manufacturing, and dosage forms, (2) animal pharmacology and toxicology, (3) human pharmacokinetics and bioavailability, (4) comprehensive results of clinical trials, (5) statistics, and (6) microbiology (in the case of anti-infective or

DRUG REGULATION AND APPROVAL

antiviral drugs).

Another important NDA or BLA component is the proposed labeling for the new drug. The label of a prescription drug is actually a comprehensive summary of information made available to health care providers. It contains the claims that the pharmaceutical company wants to make for the efficacy and safety of the drug. As part of the review process, the company and the FDA negotiate the exact wording of the label because it is the document that determines what claims the company

In addition to the directions on the bottle, prescription drugs must include labeling—package inserts or prescribing information—with detailed information for health care providers.

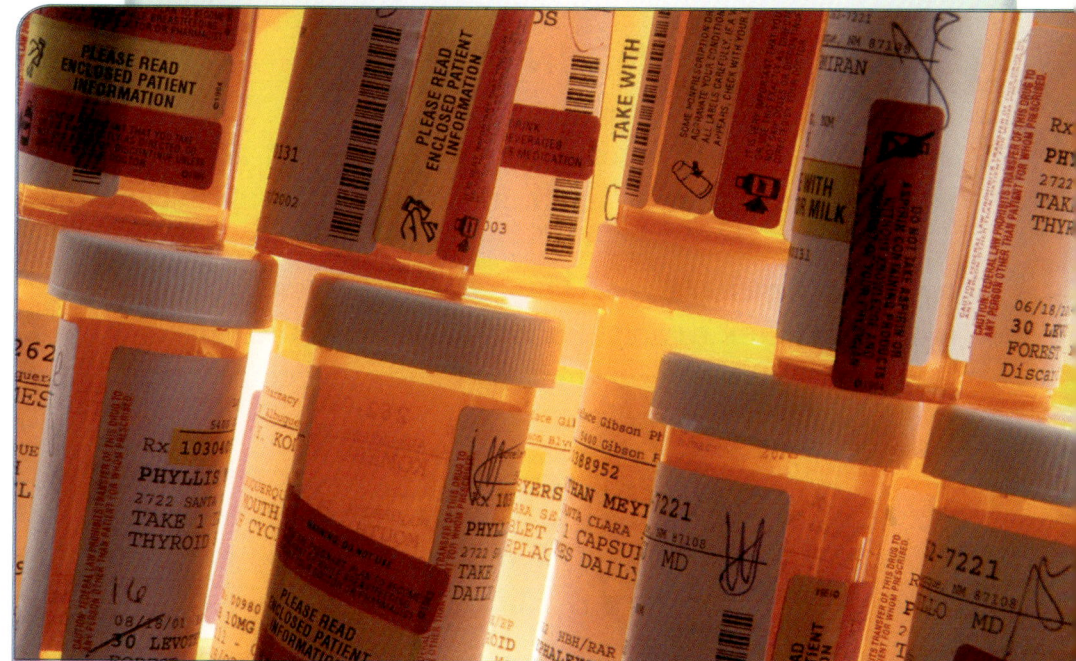

BIOPHARMACEUTICALS

legally can make for use of the drug once it is marketed.

In order for a biologics product to become licensed, the facilities in which it was manufactured and the manufacturing process itself must also meet certain standards. These include ensuring that the cell substrates used to manufacture many biologics are tested and stored properly. Although changes to the manufacturing process may not yield easily identifiable changes to a biological product, even a small change to the molecule could render it ineffective or unsafe.

Additionally, because biologics are complex, there must be a potency assay—an analysis of how effective a particular dose of a drug is likely to be in the final recipient based on the response to that dose of a drug in a predictor biological system.

SAFETY TESTING IN ANIMALS

A number of safety tests are performed on animals, prior to clinical trials in humans, in order to select the most suitable lead chemical and dosage form for drug development. The safety tests can include studies of acute toxicity, subacute and chronic toxicity, carcinogenicity, reproductive and developmental toxicity, and mutagenicity.

TOXICITY TESTS

In acute toxicity studies, a single large or potentially toxic dose of the drug is administered to animals via the intended route of human administration, and the animals are observed for one to four weeks, depending on the drug. At the end of the observation period, organ and tissue toxicities are evaluated. Acute toxicity studies generally are required to be carried out in two mammalian species prior to beginning any Phase 1 (safety) study in humans. Subchronic toxicity studies (up to three months) and chronic toxicity studies (longer than three months) require daily drug administration and usually do not start until after Phase 1 studies are completed. This is because the drug may be withdrawn after Phase 1 testing and because data on the effect of the drug in humans may be important for the design of longer-duration animal studies. When these studies are required, they are conducted in two mammalian species and are designed to allow for detection of neurological, physiological, biochemical, and hematological abnormalities occurring during the course of the study. Organ and tissue toxicity and pathology are evaluated when the studies are terminated.

The number and type of animal safety tests required varies with the intended duration of human use of the drug. If the drug is to be used for only a few days in humans, acute and subacute animal toxicity studies may be all that is required. If the human drug use is for six months or longer, animal toxicity studies of six months or more may be required before the drug is marketed. Carcinogenicity (potential to cause cancer) studies are generally required if humans will use the drug for longer than six months. They usually are conducted concurrently with Phase 3 (large-scale safety and efficacy) clinical trials but may begin earlier if there is reason to suspect that the drug is a carcinogen.

TERATOGENICITY AND MUTAGENICITY TESTS

If a drug is intended for use during pregnancy or in women of childbearing potential, animal reproductive and developmental toxicity studies are indicated. These studies include tests that evaluate male and female fertility, embryonic and fetal death, and teratogenicity (induction of severe birth defects). Also evaluated are the integrity of the lactation process and the quality of care for her young provided by the mother.

Genetic toxicity, or mutagenicity, studies have become an integral component of regulatory requirements. Since no one mutagenicity test can evaluate all types of genetic toxicity, two or three tests are usually performed. Typical mutagenicity tests include a bacterial point mutation test (the Ames test), a chromosomal aberrations test in mammalian cells in vitro, and an in vivo (intact animals) test.

PHARMACOKINETIC INVESTIGATION

In addition to the animal toxicity studies outlined above, biopharmaceutical studies are required for all new drugs. The chemical makeup of the drug and the dosage form of the drug to be used in trials must be described. The stability of the drug in the dosage form and the ability of the dosage form to release the drug appropriately have to be evaluated. Bioavailability (how completely the drug is absorbed from its dosage form) and pharmacokinetic studies in animals and humans also have become important to include in a drug development plan. Pharmacokinetics is the study of the rates and extent of drug absorption, distribution within the body, metabolism, and excretion. Pharmacokinetic studies give investigators information about how often a drug should be taken to achieve adequate blood levels. The metabolism and excretion data can also provide clues about whether a new drug will interact with other drugs a patient may be taking. For example, if two drugs are inactivated (metabolized or excreted) via the same biological process, one or even both of the drugs might have its sojourn in the body prolonged, resulting in increased blood levels and increased toxicity. Conversely, some drugs induce the metabolism and shorten the body sojourn of other drugs, resulting in blood levels inadequate to produce the desired pharmacological effect.

DOSAGE FORM DEVELOPMENT

Drugs are rarely administered to a patient solely as a pure chemical entity. For clinical use they are almost always administered as a formulation designed to deliver the

BIOPHARMACEUTICALS

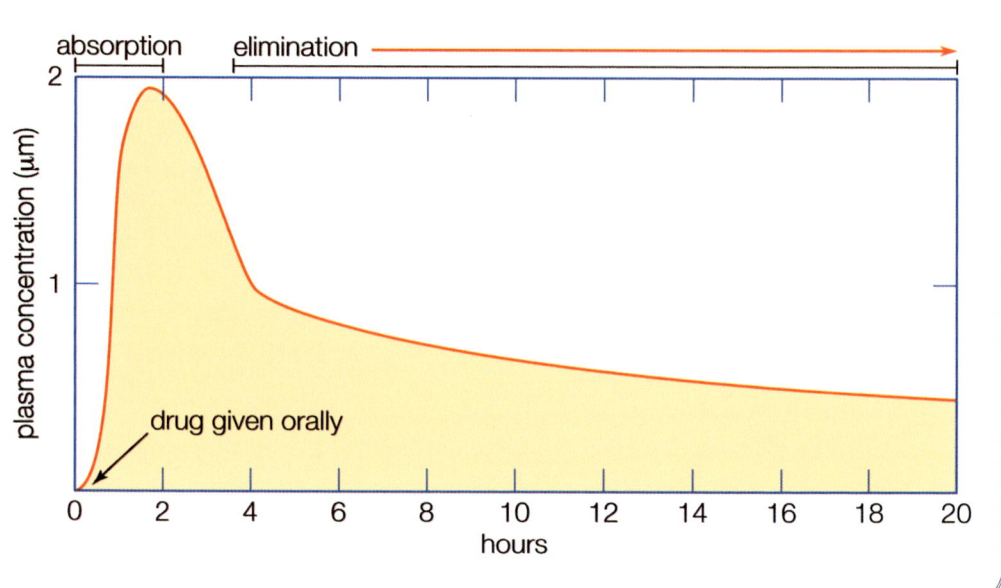

This chart represents the typical course of changes in the plasma, or blood, concentration of a drug over time after oral administration. Such data is part of pharmacokinetic investigation.

drug in a manner that is safe, effective, and acceptable to the patient. One of the most important objectives of dosage form design is to produce a product that will achieve a predictable and reliable therapeutic response. The dosage form must also be suitable for manufacture on a large scale with reproducible quality.

TABLETS

Tablets are by far the most common dosage form. Normally, they are intended for the oral or the sublingual routes of administration. They are made by compressing powdered drug along with various excipients in a tablet press. Excipients are more or less inert substances added to the powdered drug in order to (1) facilitate the tablet-making process, (2) bind the tablet together so it will not break apart during shipping and handling, (3) facilitate dissolution after the tablet has been consumed, (4)

COMMON DOSAGE FORMS

This table shows routes of drug administration and common dosage forms.

Route of administration	Common dosage forms used
oral	tablets, capsules, solutions, syrups, elixirs, suspensions, powders
sublingual (under tongue)	tablets, lozenges
parenteral (by injection)	solutions, suspensions
epidermal/transdermal (on or through skin)	ointments, creams, lotions, transdermal patches
intranasal (in nostrils)	solutions, sprays, ointments, creams
intrarespiratory (by inhalation)	aerosols
rectal	solutions, ointments, creams, suppositories
vaginal	solutions, ointments, creams, suppositories

enhance appearance and patient acceptance, and (5) allow for identification. Frequently, the active ingredient makes up a relatively small percentage of the weight of a tablet. Tablets with two or three milligrams of active drug may weigh several hundred milligrams. Tablets for oral administration may be coated with inert substances such as wax. Uncoated tablets have a slight powdery appearance and feel at the tablet surface. Coatings usually produce a tablet with a smooth, shiny appearance and decrease the likelihood that the patient will taste the tablet contents when the tablet is in the mouth before swallowing. Enteric coated tablets have a coating that is designed not to dissolve in the acidic environment of the stomach but to pass through the stomach into the small intestine prior to the beginning of dissolution. Sublingual tablets generally do not have a coating and are designed so that they will dissolve when placed under the tongue.

Tablets are traditionally referred to as pills. Prior to the widespread use of the machine-compressed tablet, pills were very popular products that usually were prepared by a pharmacist. To make a pill, powdered drug and excipients were mixed together with water or other liquid and a gumlike binding agent such as acacia or tragacanth. The mixture was made into a plastic mass and rolled into a tube. The tube was cut into small sections that were rolled to form spheres, thereby making pills. Pharmacist–produced pills fell into disfavour because they are more expensive to make than tablets or capsules and because the amount of drug released from pills varies more than from tablets or capsules.

CAPSULES

Capsules are another common oral dosage form. Like tablets, capsules almost always contain inert ingredients to facilitate manufacture. There are two general types of capsules—hard gelatin capsules and soft gelatin capsules. Hard gelatin capsules are by far the most common type. They can be filled with powder, granules, or pellets. In some cases they are filled with a small capsule plus powder or a small tablet plus powder. Typically, the small internal capsule or tablet contains one or more of the active ingredients. Soft gelatin capsules may contain a liquid or a solid. Both hard and soft gelatin capsules are designed to mask unpleasant tastes.

OTHER SOLID DOSAGE FORMS

Other solid dosage forms include powders, lozenges, and suppositories. Powders are mixtures of active drug and excipients that usually are sold in the form of powder papers. The powder is contained inside a folded and sealed piece of special paper. Lozenges usually consist of a mixture of sugar and either gum or gelatin, which are compressed to form a solid mass. Lozenges are designed to release drug while slowly dissolving in the mouth. Suppositories are solid dosage forms designed for introduction into the rectum or vagina. Typically, they are made of

BIOPHARMACEUTICALS

substances that melt or dissolve at body temperature, thereby releasing the drug from its dosage form.

LIQUID DOSAGE FORMS

Liquid dosage forms are either solutions or suspensions of active drug in a liquid such as water, alcohol, or other solvent. Since liquid dosage forms for oral use bring the drug and vehicle into contact with the mouth and tongue, they often contain various flavours and sweeteners to mask unpleasant tastes. They usually also require sterilization or addition of preservatives to prevent contamination or degradation. Syrups are water-based solutions of drug containing high concentrations of sugar. They usually also contain added flavours and colours. Some syrups contain up to 85 percent sugar on a weight-to-volume basis. Elixirs are sweetened hydro-alcoholic (water and alcohol) liquids for oral use. Typically, alcohol and water are used as solvents when the drug will not dissolve in water alone. In addition to active drug, they usually contain flavouring and colouring agents to improve patient acceptance.

Since some drugs will not dissolve in solvents suitable for medicinal use, they are made into suspensions. Suspensions consist of a finely divided solid dispersed in a water-based liquid. Like solutions and elixirs, suspensions often contain preservatives, sweeteners, flavours, and dyes to enhance patient acceptance. They frequently also contain some form of thickening or suspending agent to decrease the rate at which the suspended drug settles to the container bottom. Emulsions consist of one liquid suspended in another. Oil-in-water emulsions will mix readily with water-based liquids, while water-in-oil emulsions mix more easily with oils. Milk is a common example of an oil-in-water emulsion. In order to prevent the separation of the two liquids, most pharmaceutical emulsions contain a naturally occurring emulsifying agent such as cholesterol or tragacanth or a synthetic emulsifying agent such as a nonionic detergent. Antimicrobial agents may also be included in emulsions in order to prevent the growth of microorganisms in the aqueous phase. Emulsions are created using a wide variety of homogenizers, agitators, or sonicators.

SEMISOLID DOSAGE FORMS

Semisolid dosage forms include ointments and creams. Ointments are preparations for external use, intended for application to the skin. Typically, they have an oily or greasy consistency and can appear "stiff" as they are applied to the skin. Ointments contain drug that may act on the skin or be absorbed through the skin for systemic action. Many ointments are made from petroleum jelly. Like many other pharmaceutical preparations, they frequently contain preservatives and may also contain aromatic substances and dyes to enhance patient acceptance. Although there is generally no agreed-upon pharmaceutical definition for creams, they are very much like ointments in their use. Their composition is somewhat like that of ointments except that creams often have water-in-oil emulsions as the base of the formulation. When applied to the skin, creams feel soft and supple and spread easily.

SPECIALIZED DOSAGE FORMS

Specialized dosage forms of many types exist. Sprays are most often used to irrigate nasal passages or to introduce drugs into the nose. Most nasal sprays are intended for treatment of colds or respiratory tract allergies. They contain medications designed to relieve nasal congestion and to decrease nasal discharges. Aerosols are pressurized dosage forms that are expelled from their container upon activation of a release valve. Aerosol propellants typically are compressed, liquefied volatile gases. Other aerosol ingredients are either suspended or dissolved in the propellant. When the release valve is activated, the liquid is expelled into the air at atmospheric pressure. This causes the propellant to vaporize, leaving very finely subdivided liquid or solid particles dispersed in the vaporized propellant. Some aerosols are intended for delivery of substances such as local anesthetics, disinfectants, and spray-on bandages to the skin. Metered-dose aerosols typically are used to deliver calibrated doses of drug to the respiratory tract. Usually, the metered-dose aerosol or inhaler is placed in the mouth for use. When the release valve is activated, a predetermined dose of drug is expelled. The patient inhales the expelled drug, delivering it to the bronchial airways. Patches are dosage forms intended to deliver drug across the skin and are placed on the skin much like a self-adhesive bandage. The patch is worn for a predetermined length of time in order to deliver the correct amount of drug to the systemic circulation.

MODIFIED-RELEASE DOSAGE FORMS

Modified-release dosage forms have been developed to deliver drug to the part of the body where it will be absorbed, to simplify dosing schedules, and to assure that concentration of drug is maintained over an appropriate time interval. One type of modified-release dosage form is the enteric coated tablet. Enteric coating prevents irritation of the stomach by the drug and protects the drug from stomach acid. Most modified-release dosage forms are tablets and capsules designed to deliver drug to the circulating blood over an extended time period. A tablet that releases its drug contents immediately may need to be taken as many as four or six times a day to produce the desired blood-concentration level and therapeutic effect. Such a drug might be formulated into an extended-release dosage form so that the modified tablet or capsule need be taken only once or twice a day. Repeat-action tablets are one type of extended-release dosage form. They usually contain two single doses of medication, one for immediate release and one for delayed release. Typically, the immediately released drug comes from the exterior portion of the tablet, with the delayed release coming from the interior portion. Essentially, there is a tablet within a tablet, with the interior tablet having a coating that delays release of its contents for a predetermined time.

An additional type of extended-release dosage form is accomplished by incorporating coated beads or granules into tablets or capsules. Drug is distributed onto or into the beads. Some of the granules are uncoated for immediate release while others receive varying coats of lipid, which delays release of the drug. Another variation of the coated bead approach is to granulate the drug and then microencapsulate some of the granules with gelatin or a synthetic polymer. Microencapsulated granules can be incorporated into a tablet or capsule with the release rate for the drug being determined by the thickness of the coating. Embedding drug into a slowly eroding hydrophilic matrix can also allow for sustained release. As the tablet matrix hydrates in the intestine, it erodes and the drug is slowly released. Another type of sustained release is produced by embedding drug into an inert plastic

DRUG REGULATION AND APPROVAL

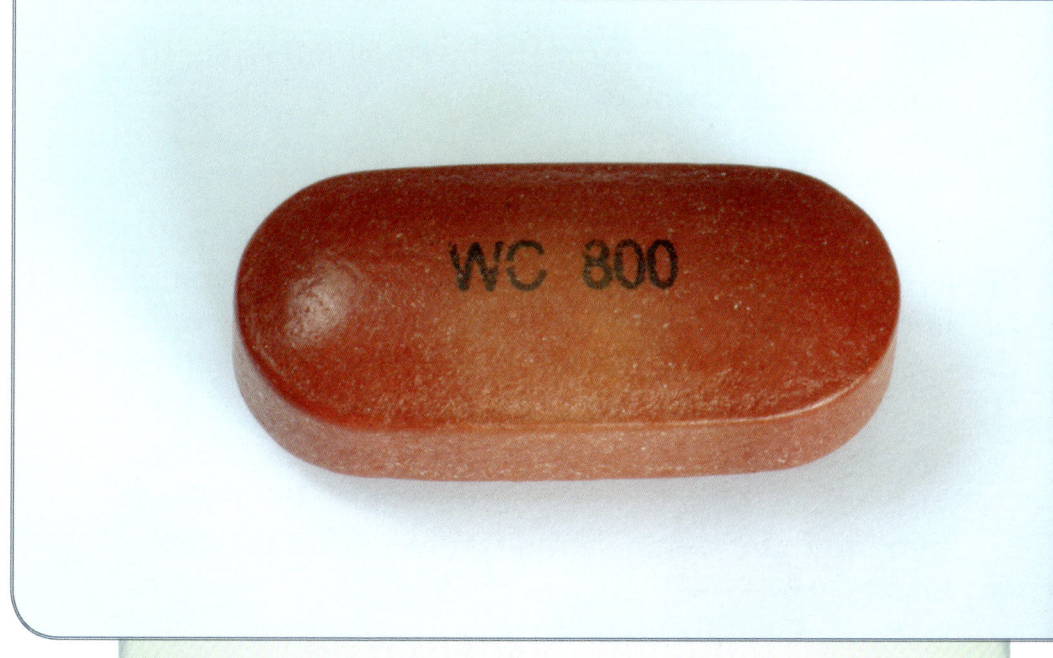

Enteric coated tablets, such as the one here, are designed to be released in the body over time while protecting the stomach from irritation by the drug.

matrix. To accomplish this, drug is mixed with a polymer powder that forms a solid matrix when the tablet is compressed by a tablet machine. The drug leaches out of the matrix as the largely intact tablet passes through the gastrointestinal tract. Drug may be adsorbed onto ion exchange resins in order to bring about sustained release. For example, a cationic, or positively charged, drug can be bound to an anionic, or negatively charged, resin. The resin can be incorporated into tablets, capsules, or liquids.

BIOPHARMACEUTICALS

As the resin passes through the small intestine, the drug is released slowly.

PARENTERAL DOSAGE FORMS

Parenteral dosage forms are intended for administration as an injection or infusion. Common injection types are intravenous (into a vein), subcutaneous (under the skin), and intramuscular (into muscle). Infusions typically are given by intravenous route. Parenteral dosage forms may be solutions, suspensions, or emulsions, but they must be sterile. If they are to be administered intravenously, they must readily mix with blood.

RADIOPHARMACEUTICALS

Radioactive dosage forms, or radiopharmaceuticals, are substances that contain one or more radioactive atoms and are used for diagnosis or treatment of disease. In some cases the radioactive atoms are incorporated into a larger molecule. The larger molecule helps to direct the radioactive atoms to the organ or tissue of interest. In other cases the diagnostic or therapeutic molecule is the radioactive atom itself. For example, radioactive iodine, such as iodine-131, can be used in thyroid studies, and radioactive gases, such as xenon-133, can be used for lung function studies. However, more often than not, the radioactive atom allows detection or imaging of the tissue of interest, and the physiological or pharmacological properties of the larger molecule direct the radiopharmaceutical to the target tissue. For diagnostic purposes, radiopharmaceuticals are administered in amounts as small as possible so as not to perturb the biological process being evaluated in the diagnosis. For therapeutic purposes, such as treatment of various types of cancer, it is the radiation produced by the radioactive atom that kills the tumour cells. As is the case for many diagnostic agents, the pharmacological effect produced by the larger molecule, into which the radioactive atom is incorporated, is of little or no consequence for the therapeutic effect of the radiopharmaceutical. Many authorities believe that monoclonal antibodies will become powerful tools for directing radiopharmaceuticals to specific tumours, thereby revolutionizing the treatment of cancer.

OBSTACLES IN DRUG DEVELOPMENT

There are many obstacles to the development of new medicines, whether they originate through chemical synthesis or biopharmaceutical processes. Many medicines that may look promising fail to live up to that promise in human trials. Others may fail safety tests, provoking adverse reactions that outweigh any possible benefit.

Even worse than medicines that fail due to adverse reactions during clinical trials are those that actually make it to market and then have to be withdrawn due to adverse reactions that only appear once the drug is in wide use in a varied population. That level of failure places severe strain on the bottom line of the company producing the drug, and of course also represents a huge human cost in the form of those affected by the adverse reactions.

Some drugs may work properly on their own, but produce unwanted effects when combined with other drugs. These kinds of drug interactions are very difficult to identify during the trial process, and most often come to light after the drug has hit the market. Physician information, labeling, and package inserts must then be modified to warn about the potential for these kinds of interactions.

Finally, there is a financial obstacle to the development of any new drug. According to the Pharmaceutical Research and Manufacturers of America (PhRMA), the revenues earned from most brand-name medicines (eight out of every ten) could not even cover the average cost of research and development.

One reason is that patent protection is fairly short-lived, after which generic versions of the medicine come to market: good news for consumers, who save money as the price of the medicine falls due to competition, but a challenge for the companies who create new medicines in the first place.

ADVERSE REACTIONS

Adverse drug events are unanticipated or unwanted effects of drugs. In general, adverse drug reactions are of two types, dose dependent and dose independent. When any drug is administered in sufficiently high dose, many individuals will experience a dose-dependent drug reaction. For example, if a person being treated for high blood pressure (hypertension) accidentally takes a drug dose severalfold higher than prescribed, this person will probably experience low blood pressure (hypotension), which could result in light-headedness and fainting. Other dose-dependent drug reactions occur because of biological variability. For a variety of reasons, including heredity, coexisting diseases, and age, different individuals can require different doses of a drug to produce the same therapeutic effect. A therapeutic dose for one individual might be a toxic dose in another. Many drugs are metabolized and inactivated in the liver, whereas others are excreted by the kidney. In some patients with liver or kidney disease, lower doses of drugs may be required to produce appropriate therapeutic effects. Elderly individuals often develop dose-related adverse effects in response to doses that are well tolerated in younger individuals. This is because of age-related changes in body composition and organ function that alter the metabolism and response to drugs.

The fetus is also susceptible to the toxic effects of drugs that cross the placental barrier from the pregnant mother. Body organs begin to develop during the first three months of pregnancy (first trimester). Some drugs will cause teratogenicity in the fetus if they are administered to the mother during this period. Drugs given to the mother during the second and third trimester can also affect the fetus by altering the function of normally formed organs or tissues. Fortunately, very few drugs cause teratogenicity in humans, and many of those that do are detected in animal teratology studies during drug development. However, animal teratogenicity screens are not perfect predictors of all human effects, so there remains some potential of drug-induced birth defects.

Dose-independent adverse reactions are less common than dose-dependent ones. They are generally caused by allergic reactions to the drug or in some cases to other ingredients present in the dosage form. They occur in patients who were sensitized by a previous exposure to the drug or to another chemical with cross-antigenicity to the drug. Dose-independent adverse reactions can range from mild rhinitis or dermatitis to life-threatening respiratory difficulties, blood abnormalities, or liver dysfunction.

POSTMARKETING ADVERSE DRUG EVENTS

Although there may have been several thousand patients enrolled in Phase 1, 2, and 3 clinical trials, some adverse drug events may not be identified before the drug is marketed. For example, if 3,000 patients participated in the clinical trials and an unforeseen adverse event occurs only once in 10,000 patients, it is unlikely that the unforeseen adverse event will have been identified during the clinical trials. Thus, postmarketing adverse-event data are collected and evaluated by the FDA. The pharmaceutical company is responsible for reporting adverse drug events to the FDA on a regularly scheduled basis. There have been many examples of serious adverse drug events that were not identified until the drug was marketed and available to the population as a whole.

Identifying adverse drug events is not always easy or straightforward. For example, the FDA may receive a few reports of fever or hepatitis (liver inflammation) associated with use of a new drug. Both fever and hepatitis can occur in the absence of any drug. If either occurs at the same time someone is taking a new drug, it is not always easy or even possible to say whether the event was caused by the drug. There are established procedures that can help determine whether the adverse event is related in a cause-and-effect manner with the drug use. If one stops taking the drug and the adverse event disappears, this suggests the event may be related to use of the drug. If the adverse event reappears when the drug is readministered, this provides even more evidence that the two events are related. However, for serious adverse events, it is often not advisable to reintroduce a drug suspected of causing the event. Because of difficulties in associating adverse events with a causative agent, these drug-induced adverse events sometimes go unrecognized for a long period of time. There have been instances when pharmaceutical manufacturers and the FDA have been criticized for failing to warn the public about an adverse drug event early enough. In some circumstances the manufacturer and the FDA had suspected that an adverse event might be caused by a drug, but they did not have sufficient data to connect the drug and the event with reasonable accuracy. This issue can be particularly difficult if the drug in question helps severely ill patients since premature or incorrect reporting of an adverse event may result in a drug being withheld from patients who are in great need of treatment.

DRUG INTERACTIONS

DRUG REGULATION AND APPROVAL

Drug interactions occur when one drug alters the pharmacological effect of another drug. The pharmacological effect of one or both drugs may be increased or decreased, or a new and unanticipated adverse effect may be produced. Drug interactions may result from pharmacokinetic interactions (absorption, distribution, metabolism, and excretion) or from interactions at drug receptors.

Interactions during drug absorption may lower the amount of drug absorbed and decrease therapeutic effectiveness. One such interaction occurs when the antibiotic tetracycline is taken along with substances such as milk or antacids, which contain calcium, magnesium, or aluminum ions. These metal ions bind with tetracycline and produce an insoluble product that is very poorly absorbed from the gastrointestinal tract. In addition, drug interactions may affect drug distribution, which is determined largely by protein binding. Many drugs are bound to proteins in the blood. If two drugs bind to the same or adjacent sites on the proteins, they can alter the distribution of each other within the body.

Interactions of drugs during drug metabolism can alter the activation or inactivation of many drugs. One drug can decrease the metabolism of a second drug by inhibiting metabolic enzymes. If metabolism of a drug is inhibited, it will remain longer in the body, so that its concentration will increase if it continues to be taken. Some drugs can increase the formation of enzymes that metabolize other drugs. Increasing the metabolism of a drug can decrease its body concentration and its therapeutic effect. Drugs can also interact by binding to the same receptor. Two agonists or two antagonists would intensify each other's actions, whereas an agonist and an antagonist would tend to diminish each other's pharmacological effects. In some interactions, drugs may produce biochemical changes that alter the sensitivity to toxicities produced by other drugs. For example, thiazide diuretics can cause a gradual decrease in body potassium, which in turn may increase the toxicity of cardiac drugs like digitalis. Finally, in the case of drugs excreted by the kidney, one drug may alter kidney function in such a manner that the excretion of another drug is increased or decreased.

While it is important to recognize that drug interactions can cause many adverse effects, it is also important to point out that there are a number of therapeutically beneficial drug interactions. For example, thiazide diuretics (which cause potassium loss) can interact with other diuretics that cause potassium retention in such a way that the combination has no significant impact on body potassium. Cancer chemotherapeutic agents are often given in combination because cellular interactions (such as inhibiting cell replication and promoting apoptosis) among the drugs cause more cancer cell death. Antihypertensive drugs are often given in combination because some of

DRUG REGULATION AND APPROVAL

the side effects produced by one drug are overcome by the actions of the other. These are just a few of the many examples of beneficial drug interactions.

DRUG PATENTS

Most governments grant patents to pharmaceutical firms. The patent allows the firm to be the only company to market the drug in the country issuing the patent. During the life of the patent, the patented drug will have no direct market competition. This allows the pharmaceutical company to charge higher prices for the product so that it can recover the cost of developing the drug and fund the development of new drugs. Virtually all drugs have brand names created by the companies that develop them. All drugs also have generic names. After the patent has expired, other companies may market the drug under its generic name or under another brand name.

Although drug patents are usually effective for about twenty years, the FDA approval process—often lasting several years—is included in that time frame, making the patent effective for an average of about twelve years after approval. Additionally, not long after a drug receives approval, its patent can be challenged. This can allow generics to come to market before the patent has expired.

The price of the patented drug usually decreases as generics come to market. The

BIOPHARMACEUTICALS

cost of developing a generic version of a drug for market is significantly less than the cost of developing the patented drug since many of the studies required for first regulatory approval of a drug are not required for marketing approval for subsequent generic versions. Essentially, the only requirement is to demonstrate that the new version is biologically equivalent to the already approved drug. Bioequivalent drug products have the same rate and extent of absorption and produce the same blood concentration of drug when the two drugs

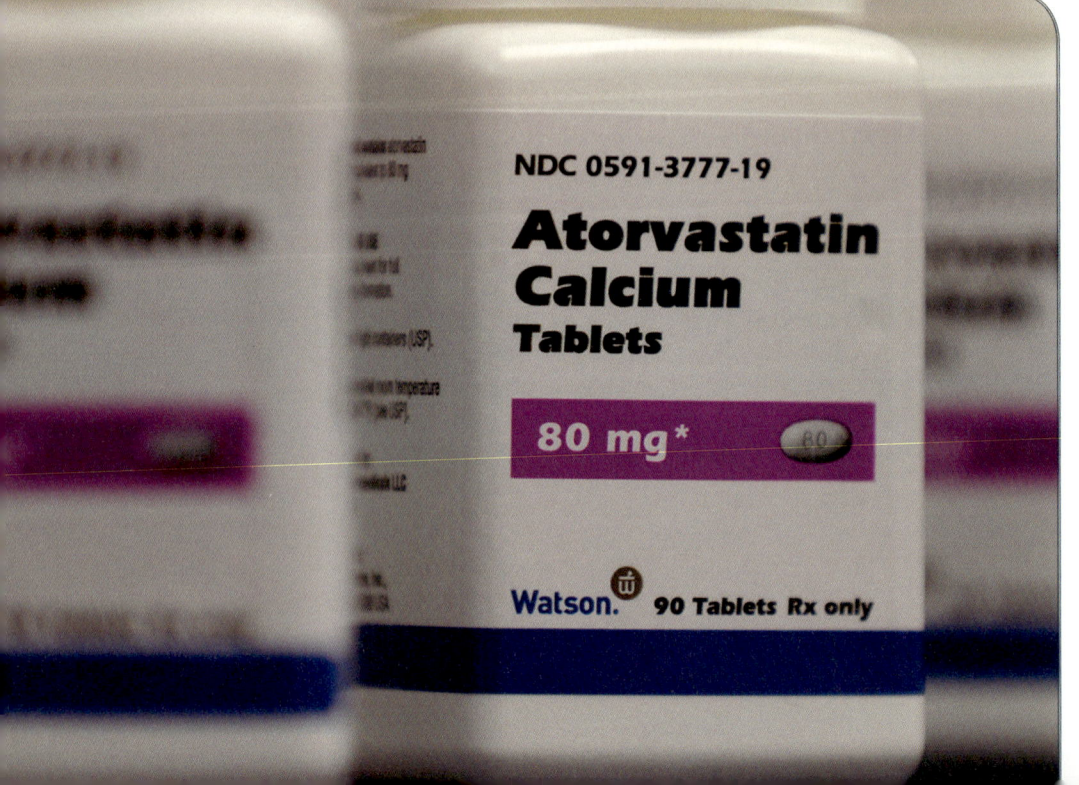

The cholesterol-lowering drug Lipitor lost its patent protection in November 2011, which opened it up to competition from the generic version, atorvastatin, seen here.

are given in the same dose and in the same dosage form.

Filling a drug prescription with a generic drug is significantly more cost-effective for most patients, which has resulted in most (approximately 84 percent, according to PhRMA) prescriptions being filled this way.

CHAPTER 4

MAJOR APPLICATIONS OF BIOPHARMACEUTICALS

Biopharmaceuticals include a wide variety of drugs, which may be derived either directly from a biological source or manufactured through the harnessing of a biological process, either naturally or through recombinant DNA technology, in which bacteria are genetically modified to produce complex biopharmaceutical molecules that normally occur in entirely different organisms.

Among the earliest biopharmaceuticals in the broadest sense was the first vaccine, created when Edward Jenner noticed that milkmaids infected with the relatively mild disease cowpox had immunity to the much more dangerous disease smallpox. In that instance, the biopharmaceutical was literally an existing life form—a bacteria that triggered an immune response that provided resistance to another bacteria.

MAJOR APPLICATIONS OF BIOPHARMACEUTICALS

Another example of a biopharmaceutical derived directly from nature was penicillin, the antibiotic properties of which were noted when a naturally occurring mold contaminated a bacterial culture.

Some of the most cutting-edge work in biopharmaceuticals continues to make use of biological material directly: cell therapy involves introducing stem cells, taken from various human sources, into damaged tissue with the goal of correcting its deficiencies. However, most biopharmaceutical products, once identified in a living organism, are then produced by introducing the genes that code for that product into bacteria that can then generate sufficient quantities of the compound for testing and, if all goes well, manufacturing of new medicines.

Some of the major applications of biopharmaceuticals in modern medicine are considered below.

ANTIBIOTICS

An antibiotic is a chemical substance produced by a living organism, generally a microorganism, that is detrimental to other microorganisms. Antibiotics commonly are produced by soil microorganisms and probably represent a means by which organisms in a complex environment, such as soil, control the growth of competing microorganisms. Microorganisms that produce antibiotics useful in preventing or treating disease include the bacteria and the fungi.

Antibiotics came into worldwide prominence with the introduction of penicillin in 1941. Since then they have revolutionized the treatment of bacterial infections in humans and other animals. They are, however, ineffective against viruses.

USE AND ADMINISTRATION OF ANTIBIOTICS

The principle governing the use of antibiotics is to ensure that the patient receives one to which the target bacterium is sensitive, at a high enough concentration to be effective but not cause side effects, and for a sufficient length of time to ensure that the infection is totally eradicated. Antibiotics vary in their range of action. Some are highly specific. Others, such as the tetracyclines, act against a broad spectrum of different bacteria. These are particularly useful in combating mixed infections and in treating infections when there is no time to conduct sensitivity tests. While some antibiotics, such as the semisynthetic penicillins and the quinolones, can be taken orally, others must be given by intramuscular or intravenous injection.

CATEGORIES OF ANTIBIOTICS

Antibiotics can be categorized by their spectrum of activity—namely, whether they are narrow-, broad-, or extended-spectrum agents. Narrow-spectrum agents (e.g., penicillin G) affect primarily gram-positive bacteria. Broad-spectrum antibiotics, such as tetracyclines and chloramphenicol, affect both gram-positive and some gram-negative bacteria. An extended-spectrum antibiotic is one that, as a result of chemical modification, affects additional types of bacteria, usually those that are gram negative. (The terms *gram positive* and *gram negative* are used to distinguish between bacteria that have cell walls consisting of a thick meshwork of peptidoglycan [a peptide-sugar polymer] and bacteria that have cell walls with only a thin peptidoglycan layer, respectively.)

ANTIBIOTIC RESISTANCE

A problem that has plagued antibiotic therapy from the earliest days is the resistance that bacteria can develop to the drugs. An antibiotic may kill virtually all the bacteria causing a disease in a patient, but a few bacteria that are genetically less vulnerable to the effects of the drug may survive. These go on to reproduce or to transfer their resistance to others of their species through processes of gene exchange. With their more vulnerable competitors wiped out or reduced in numbers by antibiotics, these resistant strains proliferate. The end result is bacterial infections in humans that are untreatable by one or even several of the antibiotics customarily effective in such cases. The indiscriminate and inexact use of antibiotics encourages the spread of such bacterial resistance.

BIOPHARMACEUTICALS

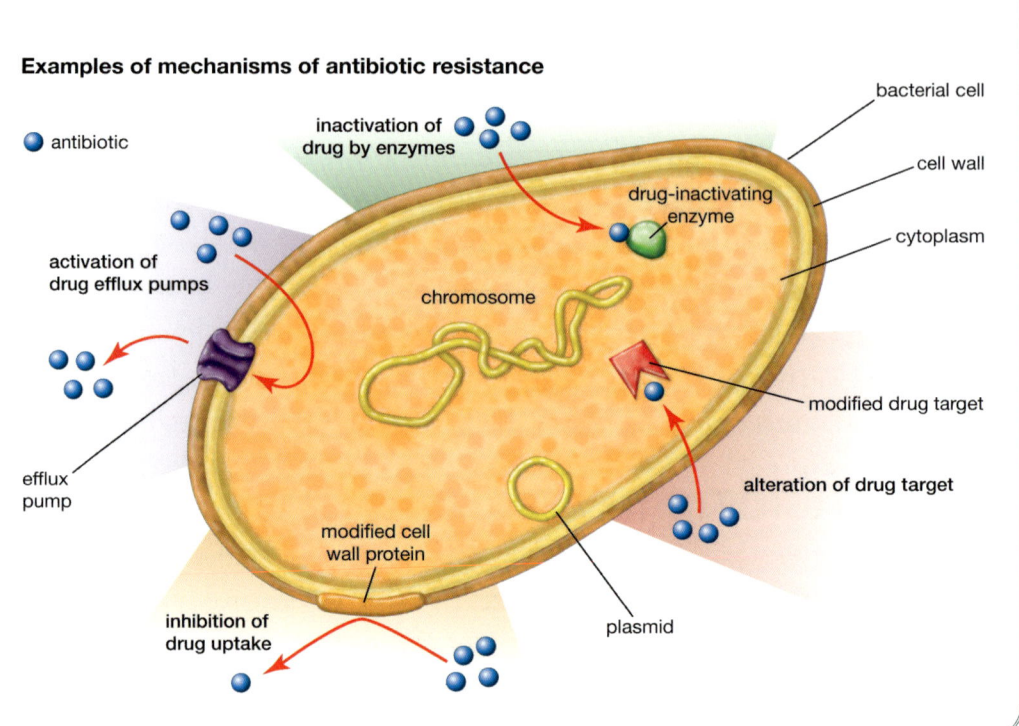

Bacteria can develop resistance to antibiotics by the activation of drug efflux pumps that actively remove a drug from the cell, the inactivation of a drug by bacterial enzymes, the alteration of bacterial cell drug targets, and the inhibition of drug uptake into the cell.

MAJOR ANTIBIOTICS

Each type of antibiotic has a specific application in medicine and can serve as a useful model for exploring the various mechanisms by which antibiotics exert their effects. The following are various types of

MAJOR APPLICATIONS OF BIOPHARMACEUTICALS

antibiotics: penicillins and cephalosporins, imipenem, the antituberculosis antibiotics, and the agents aztreonam, bacitracin, and vancomycin. These agents and groups of agents further illustrate the chemical and functional diversity found among the antibiotics.

VACCINES

A vaccine is a suspension of weakened, killed, or fragmented microorganisms or toxins or of antibodies or lymphocytes that is administered primarily to prevent disease.

A vaccine can confer active immunity against a specific harmful agent by stimulating the immune system to attack the agent. Once stimulated by a vaccine, the antibody-producing cells, called B lymphocytes, remain sensitized and ready to respond to the agent should it ever gain entry to the body. A vaccine may also confer passive immunity by providing antibodies or lymphocytes already made by an animal or human donor. Vaccines are usually administered by injection (parenteral administration), but some are given orally. Vaccines applied to mucosal surfaces, such as those lining the gut or nasal passages, seem to stimulate a greater antibody response and may be the most effective route of administration.

The discovery of vaccination is attributed to the British physician Edward Jenner, who in 1796 used the cowpox virus (vaccinia) to confer protection against smallpox, a related virus, in humans. Prior to this use, however, the principle of vaccination was applied by Asian physicians who gave children dried crusts from the lesions of people suffering from smallpox to protect against the disease. While some developed immunity, others developed the disease. Jenner's contribution was to use a substance similar to, but safer than, smallpox to confer immunity. He thus exploited the relatively rare situation in which immunity to one virus confers protection against another viral disease. In 1881 the French microbiologist Louis Pasteur demonstrated immunization against anthrax by injecting sheep with a preparation containing attenuated forms of the bacillus that causes the disease. Four years later he developed a protective suspension against rabies.

Since Pasteur's time, a widespread and intensive search for new vaccines has been conducted, and vaccines against both bacteria and viruses are produced, as well as vaccines against venoms and other toxins. Through vaccination, smallpox has been eradicated worldwide, and polio much reduced. Vaccines have also been developed for mumps, measles, typhoid, cholera, plague, tuberculosis, tularemia, pneumococcal infection, tetanus, influenza, yellow fever, hepatitis A and B, some types of encephalitis, and typhus—although some of these vaccines are less than 100 percent effective or are used only in selected population groups at high risk. Interest in bacterial vaccines slackened with the introduction

MAJOR APPLICATIONS OF BIOPHARMACEUTICALS

of antibiotics in the mid-20th century, but vaccines remain a mainstay in the fight against many infectious diseases, especially viral infections, which do not generally respond to antibiotics.

The challenge in vaccine development consists in devising a vaccine strong enough to ward off infection without making the individual seriously ill. To

Vaccination clinics around the world, such as this one in Bangui in the Central African Republic, have helped reduce the incidence of potentially deadly diseases, including measles, mumps, and typhoid, among others.

this end, investigators have devised different types of vaccines. Weakened, or attenuated, vaccines consist of microorganisms that have lost the ability to cause serious illness but retain the ability to stimulate immunity. They may produce a mild or subclinical form of the disease. Attenuated vaccines include those for measles, mumps, polio (the Sabin vaccine), rubella, and tuberculosis. Inactivated vaccines are those that contain organisms that have been killed or inactivated with heat or chemicals. These, too, elicit an immune response, but the response often is less complete. Because inactivated vaccines are not as effective at fighting infection as those made from attenuated microorganisms, greater quantities of inactivated vaccines are administered. Vaccines against rabies, polio (the Salk vaccine), some forms of influenza, and cholera are made from inactivated microorganisms. Another type is a subunit vaccine, which is made from proteins found on the surface of infectious agents. Vaccines for influenza and hepatitis B are of this type. When toxins, the metabolic by-products of infectious organisms, are inactivated to form toxoids, they can be used to stimulate immunity against tetanus, diphtheria, and whooping cough.

In the late 20th century, advances in laboratory techniques allowed approaches to vaccine development to be refined. Medical researchers could identify the genes of a pathogen (disease-causing microorganism) that encode the protein or proteins

MAJOR APPLICATIONS OF BIOPHARMACEUTICALS

that stimulate the immune response to that organism. This has allowed the immunity-stimulating proteins (called antigens) to be mass-produced and used in vaccines. It also has made it possible to alter pathogens genetically and produce weakened strains of viruses. In this way, harmful proteins from pathogens can be deleted or modified, thus providing a safer and more effective method by which to manufacture attenuated vaccines. Recombinant DNA technology has also proved useful in developing vaccines to viruses that cannot be grown successfully or that are inherently dangerous. Genetic material that codes for a desired antigen is inserted into the attenuated form of a large virus, such as the vaccinia virus, which carries the foreign genes "piggyback." The altered virus is injected into an individual to stimulate antibody production to the foreign proteins and thus confer immunity. This approach potentially enables the vaccinia virus to function as a live vaccine against several diseases once it has received genes derived from the relevant disease-causing microorganisms. A similar procedure can be followed using a modified bacterium, such as *Salmonella typhimurium*, as the carrier of a foreign gene. Another approach, called naked DNA therapy, involves injecting DNA that encodes a foreign protein into muscle cells. These cells produce the foreign antigen, which stimulates an immune response.

CYTOKINES

Cytokines are any of a group of small, short-lived proteins that are released by one cell to regulate the function of another cell, thereby serving as intercellular chemical messengers. Cytokines effect changes in cellular behaviour that are important in a number of physiological processes, including reproduction, growth and development, and injury repair. However, they are probably best known for the roles they play in the immune system's defense against disease-causing organisms.

As part of the immune response, cytokines exert their influence over various white blood cells (leukocytes), including lymphocytes, granulocytes, monocytes, and macrophages. Cytokines produced by leukocytes are sometimes called interleukins, while those produced by lymphocytes may be referred to as lymphokines.

Cytokines typically are not stored within the cell but instead are synthesized "on demand," often in response to another cytokine. Once secreted, the cytokine binds to a specific protein molecule, called a receptor, on the surface of the target cell, an event that triggers a signaling cascade inside that cell. The signal ultimately reaches the nucleus, where the effects of the cytokine are manifested in changes in gene transcription and protein expression—i.e., genes, which code for proteins, may be turned on or off, and protein production may be stimulated or inhibited.

Many different cytokines have been identified, and their activities, at least in part, are known. In some cases, one cytokine can interact with a variety of different cell types and elicit different responses from each cell. In other cases, different cytokines can elicit the same response from a cell. Some cytokines are known to induce or augment the activities of other cytokines, and sometimes their interactions occur through a cascading effect; however, the regulation of and cooperation between these various chemical signals still remain unclear in many cases. The classification of cytokines is problematic because so much remains to be learned about them, but they can be divided into five categories: interleukins, interferons, colony-stimulating factors, tumour necrosis factors, and growth factors.

Because cytokines are known to play a role in many disease processes, they have the potential to be used in treating a variety of disorders. For example, clinicians monitor levels of cytokines in the blood to assess the progression and activity of certain inflammatory states, such as septic shock. Measuring cytokine production also is useful in determining an individual's immunocompetence, or ability to fight off infection. Cytokines are used as therapeutic agents in treating persons with cancer and immunodeficiency disorders and those undergoing organ transplantation. Cytokines in conjunction with certain vaccines can enhance the vaccines' effectiveness.

INTERFERON

Interferons are any of several related proteins that are produced by the body's cells as a defensive response to viruses. They are important modulators of the immune response.

Interferon was named for its ability to interfere with viral proliferation. The various forms of interferon are the body's most rapidly produced and important defense against viruses. Interferons can also combat bacterial and parasitic infections, inhibit cell division, and promote or impede the differentiation of cells. They are produced by all vertebrate animals and possibly by some invertebrates as well.

Interferons are categorized as cytokines, small proteins that are involved in intercellular signaling. Interferon is secreted by cells in response to stimulation by a virus or other foreign substance, but it does not directly inhibit the virus's multiplication. Rather, it stimulates the infected cells and those nearby to produce proteins that prevent the virus from replicating within them. Further production of the virus is thereby inhibited and the infection is stemmed. Interferons also have immunoregulatory functions—they inhibit B-lymphocyte (B-cell) activation, enhance T-lymphocyte (T-cell) activity, and increase the cellular-destruction capability of natural killer cells.

Three forms of interferon—alpha (a), beta (b), and gamma (g)—have been recognized. These interferons have been classified into two types: type I includes the alpha and beta forms, and type II consists of the gamma form. This division is based on the type of cell that produces the interferon and the functional characteristics of the protein. Type I interferons can be produced by almost any cell upon stimulation by a

MAJOR APPLICATIONS OF BIOPHARMACEUTICALS

virus; their primary function is to induce viral resistance in cells. Type II interferon is secreted only by natural killer cells and T lymphocytes; its main purpose is to signal the immune system to respond to infectious agents or cancerous growth.

Interferons were discovered in 1957 by British bacteriologist Alick Isaacs and Swiss microbiologist Jean Lindenmann. Research conducted in the 1970s revealed that these substances could not only prevent viral infection but also suppress the growth of cancers in some laboratory animals. Hopes were raised that interferon might prove to be a wonder drug able to cure a wide variety of diseases, but its serious side effects, which include flulike symptoms of fever and fatigue as well as a decrease in the production of blood cells by the bone marrow, deflated expectations for its use against less serious diseases.

(continued on the next page)

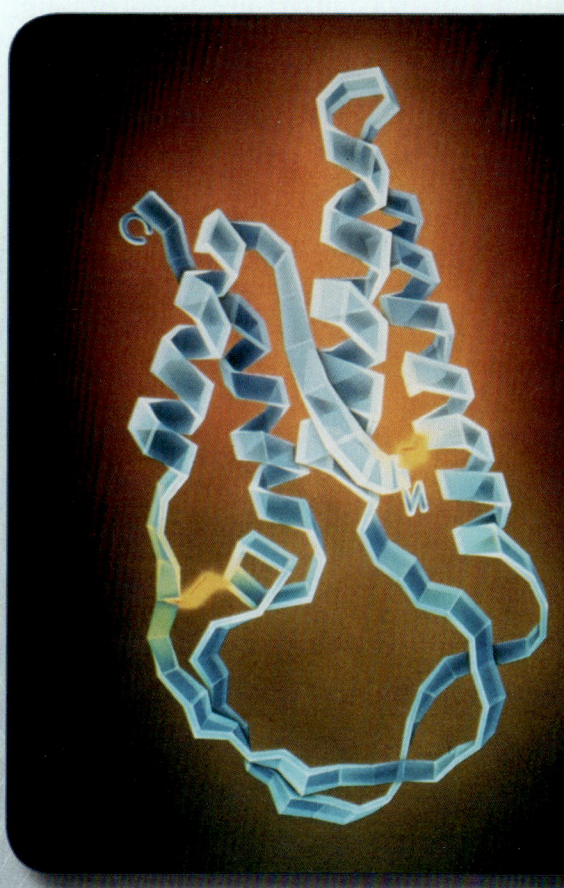

This illustration depicts a protein of interferon alfa-2B, which stems viral production in a cell and stimulates protein production in nearby cells, preventing the virus from replicating.

(*continued from the previous page*)

Despite these setbacks, in the 1980s alpha interferon came into use, in low doses, to treat hairy-cell leukemia (a rare form of blood cancer) and, in higher doses, to combat Kaposi sarcoma, which frequently appears in AIDS patients. The alpha form also has been approved for treating the viral infections hepatitis B, hepatitis C (non-A, non-B hepatitis), and genital warts (condylomata acuminata). The beta form of interferon is mildly effective in treating the relapsing-remitting form of multiple sclerosis. Gamma interferon is used to treat chronic granulomatous disease, a hereditary condition in which white blood cells fail to kill bacteria.

MONOCLONAL ANTIBODIES

Monoclonal antibodies are produced artificially by a genetic engineering technique. Production of monoclonal antibodies was one of the most important techniques of biotechnology to emerge during the last quarter of the 20th century. When activated by an antigen, a circulating B cell multiplies to form a clone of plasma cells, each secreting identical immunoglobulin molecules. It is such immunoglobulins—derived from the descendants of a single B cell—that are called monoclonal antibodies.

The antibody response to a natural infection or an active immunization, however, is polyclonal. In other words, it involves many B cells, each of which recognizes a different antigenic determinant (epitope) of the immunizing antigen and secretes a different immunoglobulin. Thus the blood serum of an immunized person or animal normally contains a mixture of antibodies, all capable of combining with the same antigen but with different epitopes that appear on the surface of the antigen. Furthermore, even antibodies that bind to the same epitope often have different abilities to bind to that epitope. This makes isolating an appreciable quantity of a particular monoclonal antibody from the polyclonal mixture extremely difficult.

HYBRIDOMA

An astonishingly high serum concentration of a single type of immunoglobulin is associated with multiple myeloma, a type of cancer in which a single B cell proliferates to form a tumorous clone of antibody-secreting cells that can multiply indefinitely, like all cancer cells (see immune system disorder: Cancers of the lymphocytes). Thus the immunoglobulins made by myelomas are monoclonal, and myeloma cells have been propagated to produce large quantities of monoclonal antibodies, which have been used to study the basic nature of immunoglobulins. Unfortunately, however, the antigen to which the myeloma antibodies bind is unknown. If an immunologist wanted to obtain large amounts of a particular antibody—say, the anti-Rh antibody—the induction of myelomas is useless, for it has proved impossible to specify beforehand what antibody will be secreted by any given myeloma.

However, it is possible to produce large amounts of a chosen, identifiable monoclonal antibody. Occasionally a cultured myeloma cell line continues to grow well but loses its ability to secrete immunoglobulin. In 1975 the immunologists Georges Köhler and César Milstein fused non-antibody-secreting cultured myeloma cells with normal B cells from the spleen of an immunized mouse. The fusion of a myeloma cell from a line that has lost the ability to secrete immunoglobulin with a B cell known to secrete a particular antibody results in a remarkable hybrid cell that produces the antibody made by its B-cell component but retains the capacity of its myeloma component to multiply indefinitely. Such a hybrid cell is called a hybridoma.

Because of hybridomas, researchers can obtain monoclonal antibodies that recognize individual antigenic sites on almost any molecule, from drugs and hormones to microbial antigens and cell receptors. The exquisite specificity of monoclonal antibodies and their availability in quantity have made it possible to devise sensitive assays for an enormous range of biologically important substances and to distinguish cells from one another by identifying previously unknown marker molecules on their surfaces. For example,

MAJOR APPLICATIONS OF BIOPHARMACEUTICALS

monoclonal antibodies that react with cancer antigens can be used to identify cancer cells in tissue samples. Moreover, if short-lived radioactive atoms are added to these antibodies and they are then administered in tiny quantities to a patient, they become attached exclusively to the cancer

The essential steps to the artificial production of monoclonal antibodies. HGPRT is hypoxanthineguanine phosphoribosyltransferase, an enzyme that allows cells to grow on a medium containing HAT, or hydroxanthine, aminopterin, and thymidine. Only hybridomas can live in the HAT medium.

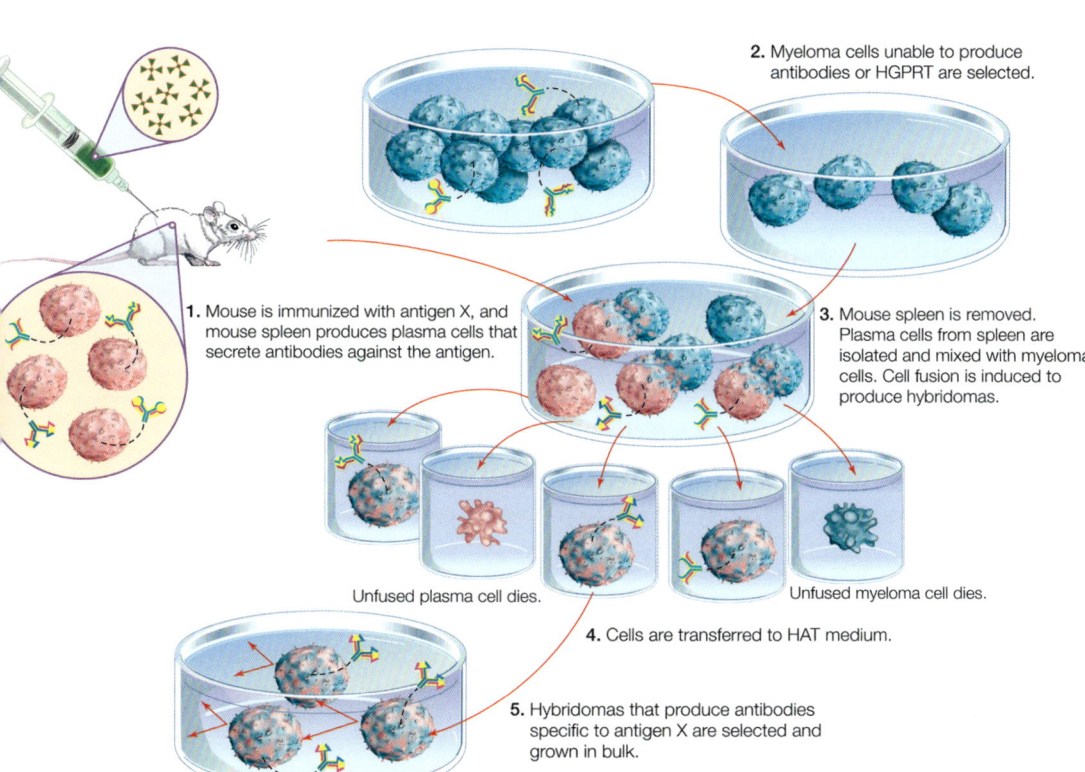

2. Myeloma cells unable to produce antibodies or HGPRT are selected.

1. Mouse is immunized with antigen X, and mouse spleen produces plasma cells that secrete antibodies against the antigen.

3. Mouse spleen is removed. Plasma cells from spleen are isolated and mixed with myeloma cells. Cell fusion is induced to produce hybridomas.

Unfused plasma cell dies.

Unfused myeloma cell dies.

4. Cells are transferred to HAT medium.

5. Hybridomas that produce antibodies specific to antigen X are selected and grown in bulk.

tissue. By means of instruments that detect the radioactivity, physicians can locate the cancerous sites without surgical intervention. Monoclonal antibodies also have been used experimentally to deliver cytotoxic drugs or radiation to cancer cells.

HUMAN MONOCLONAL ANTIBODIES

Although the preparation of monoclonal antibodies from rat or mouse cells has become routine practice, the construction of human hybridomas has not been as easy. This is partly because most human myeloma cells do not grow well in culture, and those that do have not produced stable hybridomas. If, however, human B cells isolated from blood are infected by the Epstein-Barr virus (the agent that causes infectious mononucleosis), they can be propagated in culture, where they continue to secrete immunoglobulin. Very few of them are likely to produce an antibody with a desired specificity, even from a subject who has been immunized; but in some instances immunologists have succeeded in identifying and selecting cells that secrete the wanted immunoglobulin. These cells can be grown in culture as single clones that secrete a monoclonal antibody. Researchers have used this process to obtain human monoclonal antibodies against the Rh antigen.

A simpler method of constructing human monoclonal antibodies can be accomplished using recombinant DNA techniques. Once a mouse monoclonal antibody has been constructed using the traditional methods just described, DNA encoding the antigen-binding portion of the antibody molecule can be isolated and fused to human DNA that encodes an antibody. Then the hybrid DNA is inserted into a bacterium, which produces half-mouse, half-human monoclonal antibodies. The antibodies made by this method are less likely to induce an anti-antibody response when given to humans. Further fine-tuning can be done to change all parts of the antibody that are not directly involved in binding to the specific antigen. This technique has been used to produce a large number of different monoclonal antibodies for use in therapy.

CELL THERAPY

Cell therapy involves the introduction of new cells into tissues in order to treat a disease. These are usually stem cells, which are undifferentiated cells that can renew themselves through cell division, sometimes even after long periods of inactivity. Additionally, under certain physiological or experimental conditions, they can be induced to become tissue- or organ-specific cells with special functions. Thus, every time a stem cell divides, each new cell has the potential either to remain a stem cell or become a more specialized cell.

In some organs, such as the gut and bone marrow, stem cells regularly divide to repair and replace worn

BIOPHARMACEUTICALS

out or damaged tissues. In other organs, however, such as the pancreas and the heart, stem cells divide only under special conditions. They serve as a kind of internal repair system in many tissues, dividing without limit to replenish other cells as long as the human or animal lives.

Although most stem cell therapies are still exper-

Stem cells harvested for a bone marrow transplant are incubated with antibodies that bind only to stem cells to remove unwanted cells. Once in the bloodstream, the stem cells travel to the bone marrow, where they implant themselves and begin producing healthy cells.

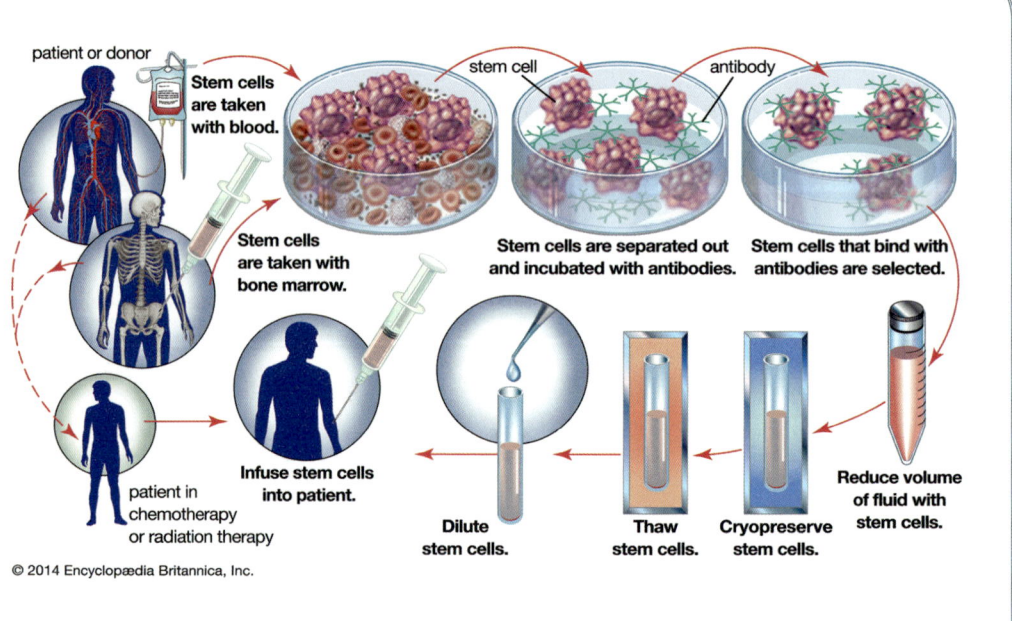

© 2014 Encyclopædia Britannica, Inc.

118

imental and costly (with the exception of the widely used bone marrow transplant for the treatment of leukemia and other blood disorders), researchers hope that one day cell therapy could be used to treat cancer, type 1 diabetes, cardiac failure, muscle damage, neurological disorders, and more.

Neural stem cells (NSCs) have the potential to give rise to offspring cells that grow and differentiate into neurons and glial cells (non-neuronal cells that insulate neurons and enhance the speed at which neurons send signals). For years it was thought that the brain was a closed, fixed system. Even the renowned Spanish neuroanatomist Santiago Ramón y Cajal, who won the Nobel Prize for Physiology in 1906 for establishing the neuron as the fundamental cell of the brain, was unaware of the mechanisms of neurogenesis (the formation of nerve tissue) during his otherwise remarkable career. There were only a handful of discoveries, primarily in rats, birds, and primates, in the latter half of the 20th century that hinted at the regenerative capability of brain cells. During this time, scientists assumed that once the brain was damaged or began to deteriorate it could not regenerate new cells in the way that other types of cells, such as liver and skin cells, are able to regenerate. The generation of new brain cells in the adult brain was thought to be impossible since a new cell could never fully integrate itself into the existing complex system of the brain. It was not until 1998 that NSCs were discovered in humans, found first in a region of the brain called the hippocampus, which was known to be instrumental in the formation of memories. NSCs were later also found to be active in the olfactory bulbs (an area that processes smell) and dormant and inactive in the septum (an area that processes emotion), the striatum (an area that processes movement), and the spinal cord.

Today scientists are investigating pharmaceuticals that could activate dormant NSCs in case the areas where neurons are located become damaged. Other avenues of research seek to figure out ways to transplant NSCs into damaged areas and to coax them to migrate throughout damaged areas. Still other stem cell researchers seek to take stem cells from other sources (i.e., embryos) and to influence these cells to develop into neurons or glial cells. The most controversial of these stem cells are the ones procured from human embryos, which must be destroyed in order to obtain the cells. Scientists have been able to create induced pluripotent stem cells by reprogramming adult somatic cells (cells of the body, excluding sperm and egg cells) through the introduction of certain regulatory genes. However, the generation of reprogrammed cells requires the use of a retrovirus, and therefore these cells have the potential to introduce harmful cancer-causing viruses into patients. Embryonic stem cells (ESCs) possess amazing potential, since they are capable of being turned into any type of cell found in the human body, but further research is needed to develop better methods of isolating and generating ESCs.

Stroke recovery is one area of research where much has been discovered about the promise and the complexities of stem cell therapy. Two main approaches can be taken to stem cell therapy: the endogenous approach or the exogenous approach. The endogenous approach relies on stimulating adult NSCs within the patient's own body. These stem cells are found in two zones of the dentate gyrus (part of the hippocampus) in the brain, as well as in the striatum (part of the basal ganglia located deep within the cerebral hemispheres), the neocortex (the outer thickness of the highly convoluted cerebral cortex), and the spinal cord. In rat models, growth factors (cell growth-mediating substances), such as fibroblast growth factor-2, vascular endothelial growth factor, brain-derived neurotrophic factor, and erythropoietin, have been administered after strokes in an effort to induce or enhance neurogenesis, thereby staving off brain damage and spurring functional recovery. The most promising growth factor in the rat models was erythropoietin, which promotes neural progenitor cell proliferation and has been shown to induce neurogenesis and functional improvement following embolic stroke in rats. This was followed by clinical trials in which erythropoietin was administered to a small sample of stroke patients, who eventually showed dramatic improvements over individuals in the placebo group. Erythropoietin has also shown promise in patients with schizophrenia and in patients with multiple sclerosis. However, further studies need to be performed in larger groups of patients in order to confirm the efficacy of erythropoietin.

Exogenous stem cell therapies rely upon extraction, in vitro cultivation, and subsequent transplantation of stem cells into the regions of the brain affected by stroke. Studies have shown that adult NSCs can be obtained from the dentate gyrus, hippocampus, cerebral cortex, and subcortical white matter (layer underneath the cerebral cortex). Actual transplantation studies have been carried out in rats with spinal cord injury using stem cells that had been biopsied from the subventricular zone (area underlying the walls of the fluid-filled brain cavities, or ventricles) of the adult brain. Fortunately, there were no functional deficits as a result of the biopsy. There have also been studies in rats in which ESCs or fetal-derived neural stem cells and progenitor cells (undifferentiated cells; similar to stem cells but with narrower differentiation capabilities) have been transplanted into regions of the brain damaged by stroke. In these studies, the grafted NSCs successfully differentiated into neurons and glial cells, and there was some functional recovery. The major caveat, however, with exogenous therapies is that scientists have yet to understand fully the underlying mechanisms of differentiation of the progenitor cells and their integration into existing neuronal networks. In addition, scientists and clinicians do not yet know how to control the proliferation, migration, differentiation, and survival of NSCs and their progeny. This is due to the fact that NSCs are partially regulated by the specialized microenvironment, or niche, in which they reside.

There has also been research into hematopoietic stem cells (HSCs), which usually differentiate into blood cells but can also be transdifferentiated into neural lineages. These HSCs can be found in bone marrow, umbilical cord blood, and peripheral blood cells. Interestingly, these cells have been found to be spontaneously mobilized by certain types of strokes and can also be further mobilized by granulocyte colony stimulating factor (G-CSF). Studies of G-CSF in rats have shown that it can lead to functional improvement following stroke, and clinical trials in humans appear promising. Exogenous studies have also been carried out in rats with HSCs. The HSCs were administered locally at the site of damage in some studies or administered systemically through intravenous transplantation in other studies. The latter procedure is simply more feasible, and the most effective HSCs seem to be those derived from the peripheral blood.

The research that has been done on stem cell therapies for epilepsy and Parkinson's disease also demonstrates the promise and difficulty of properly cultivating stem cells and introducing them into a living system. With regard to ESCs, studies have shown that they are capable of being differentiated into dopaminergic neurons (neurons that transmit or are activated by dopamine), spinal motor neurons, and oligodendrocytes (nonneuronal cells associated with the formation of myelin). In studies aimed at treating epilepsy, mouse embryonic stem-cell-derived neural precursors (ESNs) were transplanted into the hippocampi of chronically epileptic rats and control rats. After transplantation, no differences were found in the functional properties of the ESNs, as they all displayed the synaptic properties characteristic of neurons. However, it still remains to be seen whether ESNs have the ability to survive for prolonged periods in the epileptic hippocampus, to differentiate into neurons with the proper hippocampal functions, and to suppress learning and memory deficits in chronic epilepsy. NSCs, on the other hand, have already been observed to survive and to differentiate into different functional forms of neurons in rats. However, it is unclear whether NSCs can differentiate into the different functional forms in appropriate amounts and whether they can synapse properly with hyperexcitable neurons in order to inhibit them, thereby curbing seizures.

Treatments for Parkinson's disease also show promise and face similar obstacles. Clinical research has been carried out on the transplantation of human fetal mesencephalic tissue (tissue derived from the midbrain, which forms part of the brainstem) into the striata of Parkinson's patients. However, this tissue is of limited availability, which is what makes ESC transplantation more appealing. Indeed, research has already shown that transplantable dopaminergic neurons—the kind of neurons affected in Parkinson's disease—can be generated from mouse, primate, and human ESCs. The one major difference between mouse and human ESCs, however, is that human ESCs take much longer to differentiate (up to 50 days). Also, differentiation programs for human ESCs require the introduction of animal serum in order to propagate, which might violate certain medical regulations, depending on the country. Researchers will also need to figure out a way to get ESC-derived dopaminergic progenitor cells to survive for a longer period of time after transplantation. Finally, there is the issue of the purity of ESC-derived cell populations; all the cells must be certified as dopaminergic precursor cells before they can be safely transplanted. Nevertheless, differentiation and purification techniques are improving with each study. Indeed, the generation of large banks of pure and specific cell populations for human transplantation remains an attainable goal.

ENZYMES

Enzymes are complex proteins that cause a specific chemical change in other substances without being changed themselves. A number of important enzymes have been produced using rDNA technology for use in medicine.

One of the best-known is alteplase (also known as TPA, for "tissue-type plasminogen activator"). In the circulatory system, the process of dissolving blood clots involves converting the protein plasminogen to the proteolytic enzyme plasmin. Alteplase is an enzyme that accelerates this conversion, and thus can contribute to the treatment of heart attacks, strokes, and pulmonary emboli, all of which are caused by blood clots. Because alteplase's effects are more localized than those of other enzymes used to dissolve blood clots (streptokinase and urokinase), it is less likely to cause bleeding throughout the body, which poses its own health risk.

Another enzyme being produced with rDNA technology is Dornase alfa, used in the treatment of cystic fibrosis (CF), a genetic disorder that causes excessive mucous secretions and frequent lung infections. Only about half of those with CF have typically lived more than 30 years. The body produces a DNA-splitting enzyme called DNase I, which can break down DNA that is outside cells but not DNA that is inside cells. Dornase alfa, however, a recombinant variant of DNase I in aerosol form, can break down DNA inside cells. The decomposition of this DNA in the excessive mucous secretions of people suffering from CF can make the mucous secretions

MAJOR APPLICATIONS OF BIOPHARMACEUTICALS

less adhesive, which in turn reduces the risk of lung infections. Dornase alfa can thus decrease the incidence and duration of both lung infections and hospital stays in CF patients. When it came on the market in 1993, it was the first new drug the FDA had approved in 30 years for the management of CF.

Another example of an recombinant enzyme is imiglucerase, used in the treatment of Gaucher's disease, a hereditary deficiency of glucocerebrosidase (of which imiglucerase is a variant), which is characterized by bone destruction and enlargement of the liver and spleen. This enzyme can be extracted from human placentas, but it would take 20,000 placentas to provide only a year's supply for a single patient, at a cost of hundreds of thousands of dollars, and everyone with Gaucher's disease needs a lifelong supply. The FDA's approval of imiglucerase solved this supply problem.

Recombinant enzymes continue to be developed to treat other conditions. One currently being investigated is alkaline phosphatase. An inherited deficiency in this enzyme produces the bone disease hypophosphatasia, which hinders the formation of bones and teeth and can result in substantial skeletal abnormalities. Should the potential therapy in development make it to market, it would be the first medicine ever approved for this rare disease and should provide the enzyme necessary for proper bone growth in afflicted infants.

BIOPHARMACEUTICALS

HORMONES

Hormones are regulatory molecules produced by the body. In the body, true endocrine hormones are substances synthesized by a particular gland and then released into the circulatory system so they can travel to a distant sensitive cell and bring about changes in that cell. A looser definition of hormone is now being used—it considers any regulatory substance that carries a signal to generate some kind of change in a target cell to be a hormone. Under this broad a definition, all cytokines are also hormones.

However, true endocrine hormones are fairly well defined, and several of them are now being produced using rDNA technology, including insulin, glucagon, human growth hormone, and others. Insulin, already discussed in detail, was the first rDNA biopharmaceutical approved for human use.

Biologically glucagon is almost the opposite of insulin: it stimulates the breakdown of glycogen, lipids, and protein, which increases blood glucose levels. Physiologically this is important because it prevents hypoglycemia. Glucagon is also used in the treatment of diabetics since administration of too much insulin, administration of insulin prior to a meal that then isn't eaten, or increased physical activity can all bring on hypoglycemia. It also has uses as a diagnostic aid during certain radiological examinations. Much like insulin, glucagon was traditionally purified from

MAJOR APPLICATIONS OF BIOPHARMACEUTICALS

cow or pig pancreas, but it is now being produced through rDNA technology under trade names such as GlucaGen.

Another important hormone being produced by rDNA technology is growth hormone. A deficiency in the secretion of human growth hormone during the years of active growth results in pituitary dwarfism, while overproduction results in gigantism. Human growth hormone, which could previously only be extracted from the pituitary glands of cadavers, is now made using rDNA technology and thus available for various therapeutic uses: treating short stature caused by a growth hormone deficiency but also treatment of defective growth caused by various other

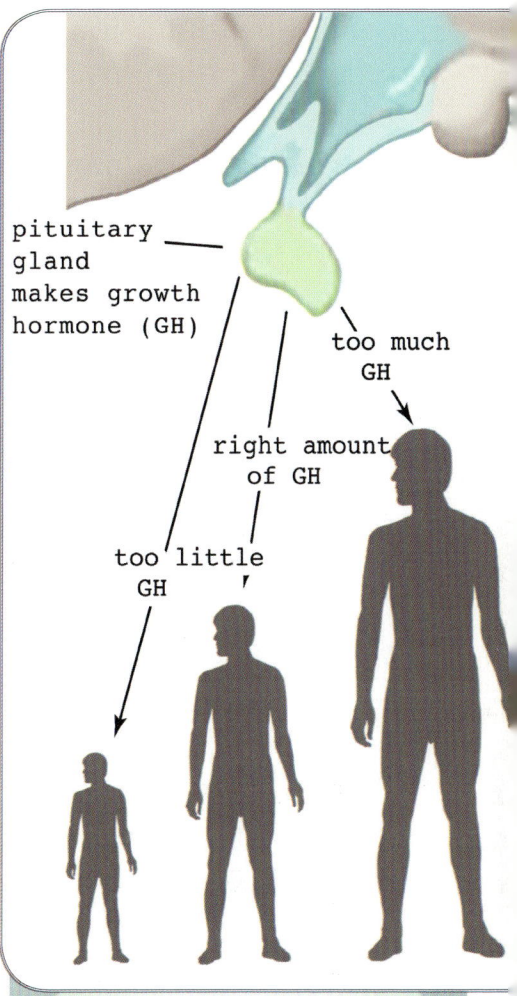

Growth hormone is secreted by the anterior lobe of the pituitary gland and is vital for normal physical growth in children. Too much results in gigantism (right), and too little results in dwarfism (left).

conditions. Additionally, it has the potential to help induce lactation, counteract the effects of aging, and more.

Other hormones that have been produced using rDNA technology include the gonadotrophins (hormones that primarily target the gonads, directly and indirectly regulating reproductive function), which among other uses help in fertility treatments and assisted reproduction; and hormones that stimulate the thyroid and bone production.

BLOOD FACTORS

Hemophilia is a hereditary disease caused by the body's failure to produce certain proteins required for blood clotting, referred to as factors. A deficiency in factor VIII produces hemophilia A; a deficiency in factor IX produces hemophilia B. One of the unusual things about the condition is that, because the genes encoding these factors are on the X chromosome, hemophilia usually affects only men, who have only one X chromosome. Women who carry the gene don't have the disease themselves because they also have a normal X chromosome, but they serve as carriers and can pass the disease on to their sons. Hemophilia is also known as the royal disease because it afflicted the royal houses of Europe, in particular the family line of Queen Victoria.

A patient suffering from severe hemophilia may

produce less than one percent of the normal amount of the affected clotting factor. Without treatment, hemophiliacs are prone to painful, debilitating, and usually eventually fatal (typically at a fairly young age) internal bleeding.

The only treatment for hemophilia, or for a bleeding episode, is to replace the missing factor intravenously. Up until the late 1960s, fresh frozen plasma was the mainstay of treatment. However, since each bag of plasma contained only tiny amounts of the blood factors needed, it took large volumes of plasma, and usually hospitalization, to treat even relatively minor bleeding episodes. Many adolescents were thus reluctant to tell their parents when they were bleeding, delaying treatment.

In the mid-1960s a method was found for preparing factor VIII from fresh frozen plasma, allowing intravenous administration of more factor VIII in a smaller volume and reducing the need for hospitalization for bleeds and even allowing for elective surgery in patients with hemophilia A. By the late 1960s, methods had been developed for separating factor VIII and factor IX from pooled plasma and storing it in freeze-dried form. This allowed hemophiliacs largely to treat themselves at home.

But the blood factors were extracted from pools of plasma derived from thousands of donations, and in the early 1980s, it was discovered that deadly blood-borne diseases like hepatitis and HIV were being spread to hemophiliacs. Manufacturers began developing methods of killing the viruses, but thousands of hemophiliacs died of AIDS contracted from tainted blood.

Ironically and sadly, the factor VIII gene was successfully cloned at the height of the tainted blood tragedy, in 1984. This allowed the production of recombinant human factor VIII. By 1992, two pharmaceutical companies had licensed recombinant factor VIII products. Cloning of factor IX was first reported in 1982, and a licensed recombinant factor IX product became available for people with hemophilia B in 1997.

Some hemophiliac patients (30 to 35 percent of people with hemophilia A and one to three percent of those with hemophilia B) have inhibitors—antibodies that inhibit or interfere with the function of factor VIII or factor IX. Scientists have developed ways to bypass these inhibitors with products such as recombinant activated factor VII, licensed in 1997. Additional products to treat inhibitors, the greatest problem in the management to hemophilia, are in development today.

The safety of recombinant clotting factors has also made prophylactic treatment possible. As recommended by the National Hemophilia Foundation's Medical and Scientific Advisory Council in 1994, increasing numbers of young boys with severe hemophilia A or B are being started on prophylaxis with recombinant factor VII or IX. These biopharmaceutical products continue to make the future brighter for those suffering from hemophilia.

ANTISENSE DRUGS

Antisense drugs are designed to inhibit the production of the abnormal or malfunctioning proteins that lie at the heart of most human diseases. Once a gene is known to cause a specific disease and that gene's genetic sequence is likewise known, it is at least theoretically possible to synthesize a molecule that will bind to that gene and inactivate it, thereby preventing the abnormal protein from being made and thus preventing its damaging effects.

The drugs are called antisense because of the way they interfere with the gene's activity. The first step in the production of any protein is the unwinding of the DNA double helix and the production of a single-stranded messenger RNA (mRNA) molecule, a sequence of nucleotides (genetic building blocks) called the sense sequence. An "antisense," non–coding RNA strand that complements the "sense" strand will disrupt its activity, preventing the protein from being made. This process is also sometimes referred to as gene silencing.

Among the antisense therapies currently available are Kynamro (mipomersen), used to treat homozygous familial hypercholesterolemia (inherited high cholesterol). In 1998, Vitravene (formivirsen) was approved to treat cytomegalovirus (CMV) retinitis, an inflammation of the retina that can lead to blindness, in AIDS patients. More recently, the first human trial using antisense therapy for a neurodegenerative disease (amyotrophic lateral sclerosis, also called ALS or Lou Gehrig's disease) was carried out. Although the treatment, which involved the injection of antisense molecules into the spinal cord, was found to be safe, research continues to see if this therapy can benefit some ALS patients.

Antisense therapies are also being investigated for Huntington's disease, spinal muscular atrophy, Duchenne muscular dystrophy and myotonic dystrophy, and for potential cancer treatment.

However, the challenges are enormous: even though antisense technology was developed more than 35 years ago, it has proven extremely difficult to translate it into useful clinical applications. The antisense drugs have to be chemically modified so they won't be broken down by enzymes and will accurately bind to their intended targets. Delivering them where needed in order to provide benefit is another challenge. Additionally, antisense products could build up in certain organs such as the liver and lead to toxic side effects. Nevertheless, the potential for antisense drugs is so great that they continue to be the focus of many biopharmaceutical researchers.

MAJOR APPLICATIONS OF BIOPHARMACEUTICALS

PEPTIDE THERAPEUTICS

A peptide is any organic substance of which the molecules are structurally like those of proteins, but smaller. Peptides include many hormones, antibiotics, and other compounds that participate in the metabolic functions of living organisms. Peptide molecules are composed of two or more amino acids joined through amide formation involving the carboxyl group of each amino acid and the amino group of the next. The chemical bond between the carbon and nitrogen atoms of each amide group is called a peptide bond.

Early biopharmaceuticals were often peptides (both penicillin and insulin are peptides), but peptides quickly lost ground to chemically synthesized molecules because they were easier to produce and administer and not so easily broken down by the body.

However, recent technological advances have sparked renewed and major interest in their usage in both diagnostics and therapeutics. New faster, more sensitive analytical methods are making it possible to identify a wealth of peptides with potential pharmaceutical use, and other advances make it possible to modify these peptides and create completely artificial variants.

In addition, new production methods have become available, including recombinant DNA technology and transgenic plants and animals. All of these developments combined have led to a surge in research into therapeutic peptides. In 2011 alone, for example, there were between 500 and 600 peptides in preclinical phases of the drug pipeline. Researchers are looking at using peptides for treating cancer, cardiovascular disease, allergies, and skin disorders. Three peptides that received approval in 2012 were designed to help treat type 2 diabetes. Peptides also hold promise for the development of novel antibiotics, new kinds of vaccines, and more.

Among the benefits of therapeutic peptides is that they are generally safer for extended therapy than small-molecule drugs because they are highly specific and typically effective at much lower doses. Once they have done their jobs, they are easily broken down by the body, and thus do not accumulate or pose challenges to the body's detoxification mechanisms like many chemical drugs.

CHAPTER 5

THE FUTURE OF BIOPHARMACEUTICALS

Biopharmaceuticals have made remarkable advances in a very short time: it has only been a little over three decades since the first recombinant biopharmaceutical came to market. For all of its success, however, the field of biopharmaceuticals is still in its infancy. While researchers continue to develop new therapies using now well-established technologies, there are always new, cutting-edge technologies that hold even more exciting promise, from gene therapy to personalized medicine to molecular farming (a.k.a. "pharming") to synthetic biology. The challenges are immense—ethical as well as technological—but the potential is amazing.

GENE THERAPY

Gene therapy is the introduction of a normal gene into an individual in whom that gene is not functioning, either into those tissue cells that normally express the gene (curing that individual only) or into an early embryonic cell (curing the individual and all future offspring).

Prerequisites for each gene transfer therapy procedure include finding the best delivery system (often a virus) for the gene, demonstrating that the transferred gene can express itself in the host cell, and establishing that the procedure is safe. Diseases for which gene-therapy research is advanced include cystic fibrosis, Huntington's disease, and familial hypercholesterolemia; research continues on its application for Alzheimer's disease, breast and other cancers, and diabetes. Some aspects of gene therapy, including genetic manipulation and selection, research on embryonic tissue, and experimentation on human subjects, have aroused ethical controversy.

PHARMACOGENETICS

Individuals do not all respond the same way to different drugs and treatments. Some respond well and get better. Some do not gain any benefit at all. And some actually get worse.

Genetic makeup has a great deal of influence on how individuals respond to drugs. By determining which genes control response to drugs, researchers hope to develop genetic tests that can predict how an individual will respond to a particular drug. If several similar drugs existed to treat the patient's condition, his or her doctor might be able to prescribe the one that a genetic test indicated would work the best and pose the lowest risk of harmful side effects.

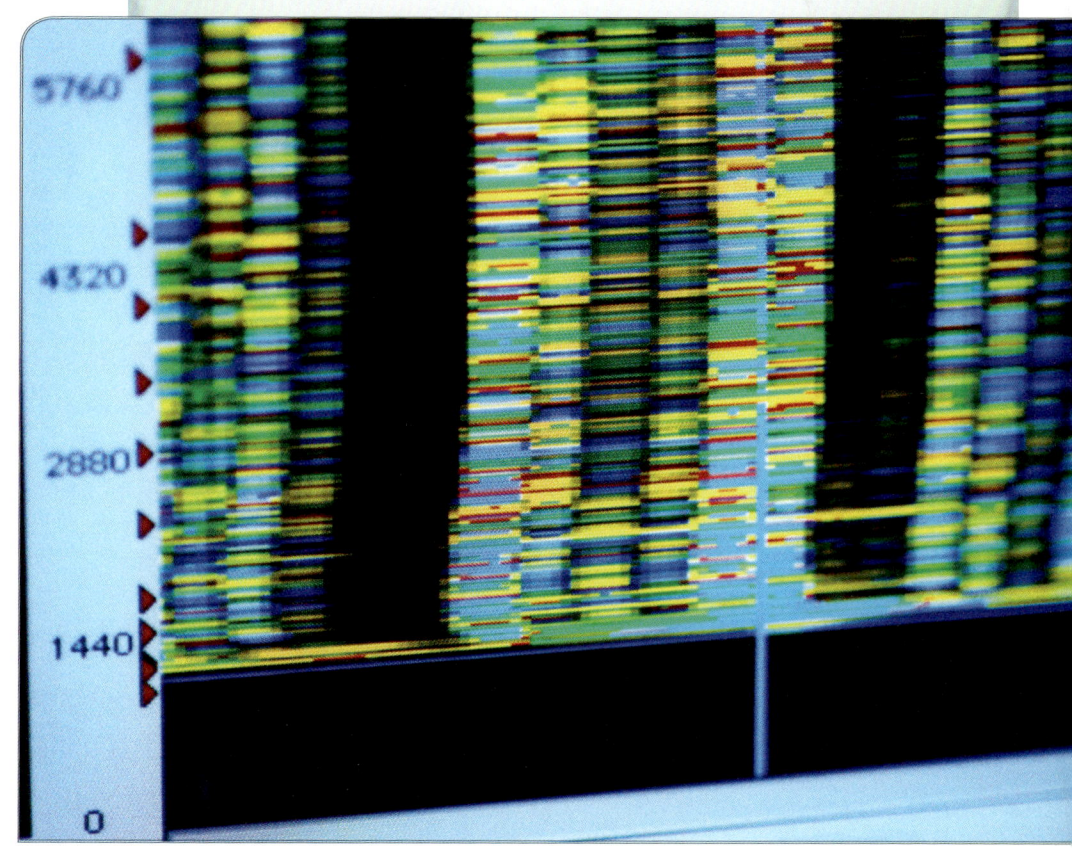

A nucleotide sequence determined using DNA sequencing technologies. Pharmacogenetic investigation has the potential to make significant progress as a result of advances in such technology.

BIOPHARMACEUTICALS

Pharmacogenetics, the study of individual reactions and interactions with drugs based on genetic makeup, is already being used in some instances. For example, people with HIV are given a test to detect their sensitivity to the antiretroviral drug Abacavir. Similarly, patients who have been prescribed the drug azathioprine, used to treat rheumatoid arthritis among other conditions, are first tested to find out whether their bodies are genetically capable of converting the drug into its active form. Some people are genetically incapable of it, and in that case the drug can build up in the bone marrow and kill developing white blood cells, which increases the risk of infections.

Breast cancer patients can be tested to see if they have mutations in a gene labeled HER2. Those who do are eligible for the drug trastuzumab (Hercaptin), which is specifically designed to interact with that gene.

Some patients with a variation of a particular enzyme do not respond well to the cancer drug tamoxifen. Cancer patients may soon be tested to find out if they are genetically compatible with it or if they would do better with an alternative drug. Pharmacogenetic tests may also soon help guide doctors in determining the safest dose of the blood-thinning drug warfarin, which can lead to dangerous bleeding if the dosage is too high.

Giving patients an individual genetic test every time they are prescribed a drug is obviously

THE FUTURE OF BIOPHARMACEUTICALS

a cumbersome and expensive proposition. Far more likely, everyone will be genetically tested early in life and that information will be stored as part of a permanent medical record so that physicians can simply refer to it to see which drugs should be given to a patient and which should be avoided.

PHARMING

The idea of genetically engineering animals and plants to produce pharmaceutical products for use in humans—a process known as molecular farming, or pharming—gained momentum in the 1980s. Producing genetically engineered plants and animals offers a more cost-effective alternative to traditional pharmaceutical development. Large quantities of biopharmaceuticals—including hormones, antibodies, enzymes, and vaccines—can be produced from a relatively small number of pharmed organisms. However, despite these advantages, pharming remains controversial due to concerns about the safety of pharmed agents and their production.

One of the first mammals engineered successfully for the purpose of pharming was a sheep named Tracy, born in 1990 and created by scientists led by British developmental biologist Ian Wilmut at Roslin Institute in Scotland. Tracy was created from a zygote (a single-celled fertilized embryo) genetically engineered through DNA injection to produce milk containing large quantities of the human enzyme alpha-1 antitrypsin, a substance used to treat cystic fibrosis and emphysema. In 1997 Wilmut and his colleagues generated another pharmed sheep named Polly, a Poll Dorset clone made from nuclear transfer using a fetal fibroblast nucleus genetically engineered to express a human gene known as FIX. This gene encodes a substance called human factor IX, a clotting factor that occurs naturally in most people but that is absent in people with hemophilia, who require replacement therapy with a therapeutic form of the substance. Polly, along with two other sheep engineered to produce human factor IX that also were born in 1997, represented a major advance in animal pharming.

The first pharmed agent produced by animals to gain approval for therapeutic use was recombinant human antithrombin (marketed as ATryn), an agent that inhibits blood clotting and that is used for the prevention of heart attack and stroke in high-risk patients. This agent is secreted in the milk of genetically engineered goats. It is then isolated and purified from the milk, which is subject to rigorous safety testing, including analysis for the presence of pathogens (disease-causing substances).

A variety of plants, including corn, rice, potatoes, tomatoes, tobacco, and alfalfa, have been investigated for their pharming potential. Plant-made pharmaceuticals (PMPs) differ from naturally occurring therapeutic plant compounds because

THE FUTURE OF BIOPHARMACEUTICALS

pharmed plants are genetically engineered to express a gene that produces a therapeutic substance. This factor also distinguishes pharmed plants from plants genetically modified for agricultural purposes. PMPs can be extracted and purified from seeds, leaves, or tubers, depending on the type of plant. An example of an agent that has been investigated for rapid production in plants is a vaccine against H_5N_1, the virus that causes avian influenza (bird flu). The production of this vaccine has been tested in several different plants, including alfalfa and tobacco. However, the need for regulations to prevent the introduction of PMPs into the environment and the food supply have proved significant obstacles to the advancement of plant pharming.

A plant biologist stands with a strain of pharmed corn grown for use in experimental research.

ATRYN

ATryn is the trade name of recombinant human antithrombin, an anticoagulant agent used to prevent thrombosis—the formation of a clot in a blood vessel that may block or impede the flow of blood, causing a potentially life-threatening condition. ATryn was developed by U.S.-based GTC Biotherapeutics and was the first therapeutic agent produced by using transgenic animals (animals whose genomes have been altered by the addition of a gene from another species) to gain approval for use in humans. The drug was approved by the European Commission in 2006 and by the U.S. FDA in 2009.

ATryn is used in patients with hereditary antithrombin deficiency, a disorder that is estimated to affect one in every 5,000 people. Antithrombin normally circulates in the blood plasma, where it binds to and inactivates certain factors involved in coagulation (the process of clot formation). People affected by antithrombin deficiency are at high risk of thrombotic events, including pulmonary embolism and deep vein thrombosis. ATryn works similarly to antithrombin and therefore serves as an effective form of replacement therapy for people with hereditary deficiency. The most common side effects associated with ATryn include headache, hemorrhage at the site of infusion, allergic reaction, and nausea.

The transgenic animals designed to produce ATryn are goats whose genomes have been altered for the secretion of human antithrombin protein in their milk. Using recombinant DNA technology, scientists were able to attach the protein-coding region of the human antithrombin gene to a segment of DNA from a goat mam-

THE FUTURE OF BIOPHARMACEUTICALS

mary gland gene that directs the release of the gene product into milk. The resulting recombinant gene, called a transgene, was then inserted into cells grown in cell culture in a laboratory. This enabled gene activity to be evaluated and cells containing the transgene to be generated for the subsequent production of transgenic animals.

Transgenic goats for breeding and herd propagation were developed by means of cloning technology based on the process of nuclear transfer—the introduction of a cell nucleus into an egg cell that has been enucleated and thus no longer possesses a nucleus of its own. Nuclear transfer was performed by fusing the transgene-containing cells grown in culture with egg cells from female goats. The eggs were fertilized, and the resulting embryos were implanted into surrogate mothers. The first-generation founder goats were then bred to give rise to female "production" goats, which serve as the main sources of Atryn. Goats in the ATryn herd undergo regular testing for activity of the human antithrombin gene; those goats with the highest levels of gene activity and therefore the highest quantities of antithrombin production are selected for breeding.

A transgenic goat whose milk will be useful in the development of biopharmaceuticals.

While pharming has many technical and economic advantages that make it commercially attractive, the issues around safety and public opinion are likely to continue to hold it back from wide acceptance. Pharming is most likely to take off in certain niche markets: for instance, to provide rapid-response vaccines, which might even be delivered orally via genetically modified cereal seeds. Further technological developments will open up new possibilities for pharming and ensure that despite the challenges, it will continue to be an exciting and innovative component of the biopharmaceutical market.

SYNTHETIC BIOLOGY

Synthetic biology makes use of many different scientific techniques and approaches in order to create functional biological systems—ones that do not naturally exist as well as redesigns of naturally occurring biological entities—from DNA, proteins, and other organic molecules. Its objective is to create synthetic biological entities that can be manipulated without producing as many complications and safety concerns as the manipulation of naturally occurring biological entities. These systems would be like factories or computers, used to create a range of products—anything from drugs to complete synthetic organisms such as complex bacteria that can digest and neutralize toxic chemicals.

THE FUTURE OF BIOPHARMACEUTICALS

Experiments with genetic engineering and recombinant DNA technology—involving the modification of the genetic code of naturally occurring bacteria by inserting single wild-type genes that could alter bacterial function—began in the 1970s. This technology led to the production of biologic drugs, agents made from proteins and other organic compounds produced by bacteria with recombinant DNA; one such compound is synthetic insulin. However, because genetic engineering uses existing genes and bacteria, it has technical limitations and is expensive.

In the early 1970s, paralleling developments in genetic engineering, scientists discovered ways to manufacture customized genes, which were built from scratch, or de novo (Latin for "anew"), one nucleotide (one unit of DNA) at a time. Throughout the 1980s and '90s and in the early 2000s, DNA synthesis technologies became increasingly efficient, in both cost and time, thereby enabling steady advance and more ambitious experimentation. By manufacturing novel stretches of DNA, scientists have been able to create de novo organic compounds efficiently that are more complex than those that occur in nature and that are better suited for specific purposes.

ADVANCES IN SYNTHETIC BIOLOGY

A breakthrough in synthetic biology came in June 2007. Scientists at the J. Craig Venter Research Institute

(JCVI) in the United States successfully transplanted the entire genome of one species of bacterium (*Mycoplasma mycoides*) into the cytoplasm of another (*Mycoplasma capricolum*), accomplishing the first full genome transplant. The new bacteria were completely devoid of their native genes and, after cell division, became phenotypically equivalent (similar in their observable characteristics) to *M. mycoides*.

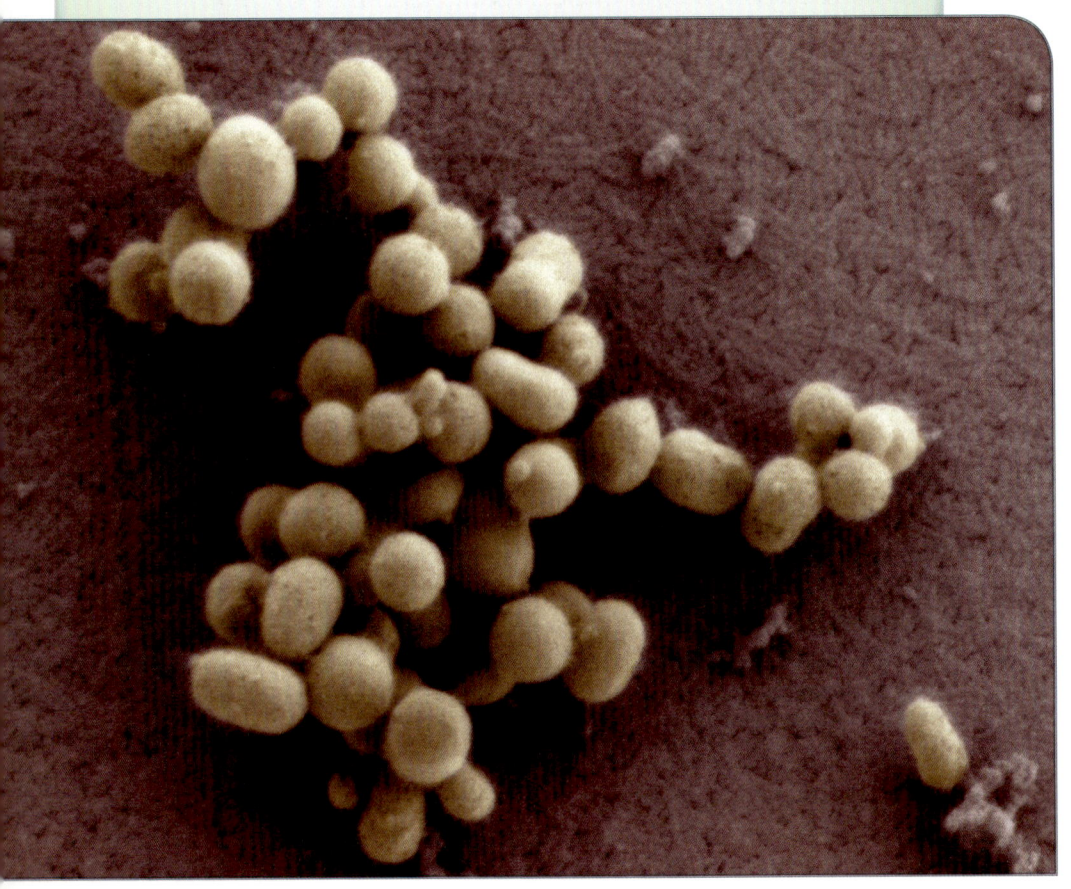

A scanning electron micrograph of cells of Mycoplasma mycoides *JCVI-syn1.0*—a synthetic bacterium.

THE FUTURE OF BIOPHARMACEUTICALS

In January 2008, JCVI scientists Daniel G. Gibson and Hamilton O. Smith successfully assembled a modified version of the genome of the bacterium *M. genitalium* from scratch. This was markedly different from the one-by-one gene modifications of recombinant DNA research since numerous genes were linked together to create a new genome. The synthetic genome was only slightly different from the natural one; the slight differences kept the genome from becoming pathogenic (disease causing) and also allowed it to be identified as artificial. The scientists dubbed this new version *M. genitalium* JCVI-1.0. Having 582,970 base pairs, it was 10 times longer than any previously assembled genome. *M. genitalium* JCVI-1.0 was created from 101 custom-made, overlapping "cassettes," each of which was 5,000 to 7,000 nucleotides long. *M. genitalium* was chosen for the experiment because it is the simplest naturally occurring bacterium that can be grown in vitro (under laboratory conditions); its genome is made up of only 482 genes (plus 43 RNA-coding genes).

The scientists at JCVI hypothesized that about 100 more genes could be removed from the *M. genitalium* JCVI-1.0 genome without sacrificing its function (although they were not sure which 100 genes). A genome of approximately 381 genes is believed to be the minimum size necessary to sustain life. The researchers planned to create this abbreviated genome, which they would then insert into a cell, thereby creating an artificial life-form. They planned to call this life-form *M. laboratorium*, and they filed a patent application for it. *M. laboratorium* would be used as a chassis upon which other genes could be added to create customized bacteria for numerous purposes, including as new forms of fuel or as environmental cleaners, capable of removing pollutants from soil, air, or water.

In May 2010, JCVI researchers announced that they had created a 1.08-million-base-pair synthetic genome and inserted it into the cytoplasm of a bacterium, making the first functioning life-form with a synthetic genome. This genome was almost identical to the naturally occurring genome of *M. mycoides*, except that it had certain genetic "watermarks" to indicate its synthetic composition.

Another scientist prominent in the field of synthetic biology was American bioengineer Drew Endy, who founded the nonprofit BioBricks Foundation. Endy was developing a catalogue of information needed to synthesize basic biological parts, or "bricks," from DNA and other molecules. Other scientists and engineers were able to use this information to build whatever biological products they wanted, knowing that certain "bricks" would consistently carry out the same function in larger organic constructions. It was Endy's hope that the BioBricks would do for bioengineering what resistors and transistors did for electrical engineering. Still other scientists attempted to create synthetic DNA with an expanded genetic code that included new base pairs in addition to the naturally occurring pairs of A-T (adenine-thymine) and C-G (cytosine-guanine).

A variation on the theme of synthetic DNA entails the synthesis of nucleic acids that carry the natural base pairs of DNA but possess a backbone made with sugars other than deoxyribose. These molecules, known as xeno-nucleic acids (XNAs), cannot be replicated by the enzyme DNA polymerase, which catalyzes the synthesis of DNA. Instead, their replication requires specially engineered enzymes, the first of which that were capable of faithfully transcribing DNA into the desired XNA product were reported in 2012.

APPLICATIONS OF SYNTHETIC BIOLOGY

Synthetic biology holds the potential to transform biotechnology, especially in such areas as the development of biofuels and pharmaceuticals. The antimalarial drug artemisinin is one example of a pharmaceutical that has benefitted from the application of synthetic biology. Artemisinin occurs naturally in the sweet wormwood plant (*Artemisia annua*), but the species grows slowly. Synthetically manufacturing the drug has yielded some 10 million times the output that was possible in the late 1990s.

Scientists were able to do this by separating the plant's DNA sequences and protein pathways that produce artemisinin and combining them with yeast and bacteria.

Other scientists have gone beyond this "cell factory" approach, which is still similar to the work done with recombinant DNA, by trying to create new forms of bacteria that can destroy tumours. The Defense Advanced Research Projects Agency (DARPA) of the U.S. Department of Defense has experimented with the creation of biological computers, and other military scientists are trying to engineer proteins and gene products from scratch that will act as targeted vaccines or cures.

BIOETHICAL CONSIDERATIONS

Like every other scientific discipline, the field of biopharmaceuticals—or, more broadly, biotech healthcare—faces the challenge of ethical considerations. In an article in the magazine *Biotechnology Healthcare*, archived at the National Center for Biotechnology Information (NCBI), the five most pressing issues in biotech healthcare were identified as:

1. Protecting human subjects in clinical trials. After a gene therapy trial at the University of Pennsylvania in 1999 resulted in the death of an 18-year-old participant, Jesse Gelsinger, univer-

THE FUTURE OF BIOPHARMACEUTICALS

sities were prompted to implement new standards designed to protect those taking part in clinical trials of new therapies. This is a complicated issue because patients who may be suffering from an illness for which no existing therapy exists are often willing to try anything new: an understandable willingness to take risks that must be tempered by rigorous protection from review committees, who must be up-front and honest about the fact that potential side effects are not known.

2. Affordability. The cost of health care is constantly rising, and many new biotech treatments for chronic illnesses are much more expensive than well-established drugs. A cholesterol-lowering pill might cost $3 a day, or about $1,100 a year. A new biopharmaceutical could cost $20,000 a year or more. This leads to ethical considerations of how much to charge for a new treatment, whether insurance companies will cover the cost, and what happens when a patient on an expensive—and potentially life-saving—new drug runs out of a means to pay for it.

3. Privacy. As we develop the ability to decipher each person's genetic composition, privacy issues come to the forefront. Does a prospective employer have the right to know that a job applicant has a genetic

BIOPHARMACEUTICALS

predisposition toward a serious heart ailment later in life? If an insurer knows that a particular patient has a genetic condition that could cost $1 million to treat with the latest biopharmaceutical treatments, what does it do with that knowledge? What if the insurer is the government, which has a responsibility not only to the patient but also to taxpayers? Who has the right to know what a patient's tests reveal?

4. Stem cell research. One of the sources of stem

A researcher holds a frozen batch of embryonic stem cells. Although restrictions on the use of embryonic stem cells in research have eased, ethical controversy over their use remains.

cells is embryos harvested from fertility clinics. The potential rewards of stem cell research are immense, but many believe that harvesting stem cells from human embryos cannot be ethical because it necessarily involves destroying those embryos. This is a debate that is unlikely to go away soon.

5. Defending against bioterrorism. The government wants to develop treatments, including medications and vaccines, that would be available in sufficient quantities to protect the largest number of people in the event that terrorists succeed in harnessing biotechnology to create bioweapons. While citizens want protection from bioterrorism, the ethical questions arise in whether funding spent on that kind of research would be better spent on other kinds of research into biopharmaceuticals and other biotech medicine.

These categories encompass the most widespread ethical concerns for biotech medicine, but there are many others. Of continuing concern are questions about the allocation of natural and financial resources. Is it ethical to use prime farmland to produce biopharmaceuticals instead of food? Is it ethical to create new forms of life that could some day pose a threat to the natural environment? Is it ethical to focus research dollars on targets that offer the greatest possibility of monetary reward for the pharmaceutical company as opposed to those that might help fewer people who are suffering from currently untreatable diseases?

The debates will continue, and although they may be raucous at times, they are also the sign of an active and growing new field of medical endeavour. After all, even Edward Jenner faced detractors as he promoted his smallpox vaccine.

CONCLUSION

Throughout history, humans have sought medicines to ease the illnesses and disorders all flesh is heir to. The advent of the scientific era launched a whole new approach to medicine, as a concerted effort was made to develop new and more effective drugs and as the germ theory of disease and other advances in basic understanding pointed the way toward better methods of treating and controlling illness.

From the earliest days of medicine, biopharmaceuticals—drugs derived from living things—have been a key part of physicians' list of remedies. While in the 20th century the focus was largely on the chemical synthesis of new compounds to treat illness, biopharmaceuticals still made their presence felt, with the discovery of insulin, penicillin, and others.

In the latter half of the 20th century that focus began to shift, as researchers learned more and more about the genetic makeup of both humans and the pathogens that produce disease. The ability to reach into organisms and directly manipulate their genetic makeup has made biopharmaceuticals the most vibrant component of modern medical research. Remarkable strides that have saved lives have already been made and improved the quality of life for millions of people. Researchers continue to learn more and more about the mechanisms of disease and how to use biotechnology to produce the proteins, enzymes, hormones, and more that battle those mechanisms.

The cost of developing these new therapies is immense and the process is time-consuming. Not all promising avenues of research pan out. Most new drugs fail to make it to market. And yet, great advances have been and are continuing to be made.

Diseases and disorders are the result of biological processes gone awry. What could make more sense than using biological processes to correct them? The future of biopharmaceuticals, it seems clear, is nothing less than the future of medicine itself.

GLOSSARY

AGONIST A chemical substance (as a drug) capable of combining with a receptor on a cell and initiating the same reaction or activity typically produced by the binding of an endogenous substance.

ANTAGONIST A chemical that acts within the body to reduce the physiological activity of another chemical substance (as an opiate); especially one that opposes the action on the nervous system of a drug or a substance occurring naturally in the body by combining with and blocking its nervous receptor.

ASSAY Analysis (as of an ore or drug) to determine the presence, absence, or quantity of one or more components; also, a test used in this analysis.

CHEMOTHERAPY The use of chemical agents in the treatment or control of disease (as cancer) or mental illness.

EXOGENOUS Caused by factors (as food or a traumatic factor) or an agent (as a disease-producing organism) from outside the organism or system.

FACTOR A substance that functions in or promotes the function of a particular physiological process or bodily system.

FIBROBLAST A connective-tissue cell of mesenchymal origin that secretes proteins and especially molecular collagen from which the extracellular fibrillar matrix of connective tissue forms.

GROWTH FACTOR A substance (such as vitamin B12 or an interleukin) that promotes growth and especially cellular growth.

IMMUNOGLOBULIN Antibody.

ISLET A small isolated mass of one type of tissue within a different type: specifically, islet of Langerhans.

MACROMOLECULE Any very large molecule, composed of much larger numbers (hundreds or thousands) of atoms than ordinary molecules.

MOLECULAR WEIGHT The mass of a molecule that may be calculated as the sum of the atomic weights of its constituent atoms.

MUTAGENICITY The capacity to induce mutations.

MUTATION A relatively permanent change in hereditary material involving either a physical change in chromosome relations or a biochemical change in the codons that make up genes.

PHARMACOGENETICS The study of the interrelation of hereditary constitution and response to drugs.

PHARMACOKINETIC Of or relating to the characteristic interactions of a drug and the body in terms of its absorption, distribution, metabolism, and excretion.

PLASMID An extrachromosomal ring of DNA that replicates autonomously and is found especially in bacteria.

PLURIPOTENT Not fixed as to developmental potentialities; especially, capable of differentiating into one of many cell types.

PRECURSOR A substance, cell, or cellular component from which another substance, cell, or cellular component is formed.

GLOSSARY

RECOMBINANT DNA TECHNOLOGY Recombining of DNA molecules from two different species that are inserted into a host organism to produce new genetic combinations that are of value to science, medicine, agriculture, or industry.

RESTRICTION ENZYME Any of various enzymes that cleave DNA into fragments at specific sites in the interior of the molecule and are often used as tools in molecular analysis.

STEM CELL An unspecialized cell that gives rise to differentiated cells.

TERATOGENICITY The capacity to cause developmental malformations.

TRANSGENIC Being or used to produce an organism or cell of one species into which one or more genes of another species have been incorporated.

VARIOLATION The deliberate inoculation of an uninfected person with the smallpox virus (as by contact with pustular matter) that was widely practiced before the era of vaccination as prophylaxis against the severe form of smallpox.

BIBLIOGRAPHY

PHARMACEUTICAL INDUSTRY

Albert S. Lyons and R. Joseph Petrucelli II, *Medicine: An Illustrated History* (1978, reprinted in 1987), provides a historical account of important developments in medicine and pharmacy through the 20th century. John C. Krantz, Jr., *Historical Medical Classics Involving New Drugs* (1974), presents a series of short stories about important drug developments with emphasis on the individuals primarily responsible for those developments. Jordan Goodman and Vivien Walsh, *The Story of Taxol: Nature and Politics in the Pursuit of an Anti-cancer Drug* (2001), describes how taxol was discovered, developed, manufactured, and marketed. Ramakrishna Seethala and Prabhavathi B. Fernandes (eds.), *Handbook of Drug Screening* (2001), provides details concerning the drug screening processes used by the pharmaceutical industry. Richard A. Guarino (ed.), *New Drug Approval Process: The Global Challenge*, 3rd ed. (2000), describes how to develop new drugs and obtain regulatory approval in global markets. Michael E. Aulton (ed.), *Pharmaceutics: The Science of Dosage Form Design*, 2nd ed. (2002), provides a detailed description of dosage forms and how they are manufactured. Sauwakon Ratanawijitrasin and Eshetu Wondemagegnehu, *Effective Drug Regulation: A Multicountry Study* (2002), compares and summarizes drug regulation in representative countries around the world.

BIBLIOGRAPHY

EDWARD JENNER

William LeFanu, *A Bibliography of Edward Jenner*, 2nd ed. (1985), is the definitive study of his writings. Sound and popularly written biographies include F. Dawtrey Drewitt, *The Life of Edward Jenner*, 2nd ed. (1933); Dorothy Fisk, *Dr. Jenner of Berkeley* (1959); Paul Saunders, *Edward Jenner: The Cheltenham Years, 1795–1823* (1982); and Richard B. Fisher, *Edward Jenner, 1749–1823* (1991). The general medical background of the 18th century is explored in Lester S. King, *The Medical World of the Eighteenth Century* (1958, reissued 1971). Derrick Baxby, *Jenner's Smallpox Vaccine: The Riddle of Vaccinia Virus and Its Origin* (1981), explores the biology of the virus in a clearly written fashion.

SYNTHETIC BIOLOGY

An introduction to synthetic biology that discusses the technologies and ethical implications of the field is Markus Schmidt et al. (eds.), *Synthetic Biology: The Technoscience and Its Societal Consequences* (2009). An exploration of synthetic biology and its meaning in the contexts of science and life is Edward Regis, *What Is Life? Investigating the Nature of Life in the Age of Synthetic Biology* (2008).

INDEX

A

acinar cells, 26, 27
adverse reactions, 38–39, 88, 89–91, 140
   postmarketing, 91–93
aerosols, 77, 82, 83, 126
agonists, 46, 54, 55, 94
allergies, 3, 82, 135–136
amyotrophic lateral sclerosis (ALS), 133–134
anesthetics, 10, 12, 18–19, 83
angiotensin, 45
   I, 45–46
   II, 45–46
antagonists, 46, 54, 55, 94
antibiotics, 8–9, 30, 36–37, 49, 93, 99–100, 101, 102–103, 104–105, 135, 136
   antibiotic resistance, 101
   categories of, 100–101
   major, 102–103
   use of, 100
antigens, 106–107, 112–113, 114, 116, 117
anti-infective drugs
   development of, 21–22
antisense drugs, 133–134
antiseptics
   discovery of, 12–13
apothecaries, 3–4, 7, 8, 17
arsphenamine, 21, 47, 54
artemisinin, 151, 152
atropine, 8, 10, 49
ATryn, 142, 144–145

B

Banting, Frederick, 26, 27–28
Best, Charles H., 27–28
bioavailability, 70, 75
bioethical considerations, 152–156
biological transport process, 44–45, 49
Biologics License Application (BLA), 70–72
biopharmaceutical industry, 34–35, 40–41, 57
biotech company, 37, 39, 41, 42
blood factors, 130–132
Boyer, Herbert W., 36, 37–38

C

cancer, 30, 33, 111, 113
   antisense therapy used to treat, 134
   drug development for, 32–33, 50–51, 53, 58–59, 63, 73–74, 87, 95, 109, 111, 112, 114–115, 135–136
   gene therapy used to treat, 138, 140
   stem cell therapy used to treat, 118
   viruses that cause, 120
capsules, 77, 78–79, 83–85, 86
carcinogenicity, 72, 73–74
cardiovascular disease, 30, 32, 45, 135–136
chemotherapy, 21, 30, 33, 95

INDEX

cocaine, 10, 18, 49
Cohen, Stanley N., 36, 37
Collip, James B., 27–28
combinatorial chemistry, 47, 56–57
cortisol, 25, 49
cortisone, 8–9
creams, 77, 81, 82
Crick, Francis, 34–35
cystic fibrosis (CF), 126, 138, 141–142
cytokines, 107–109, 110, 128

D

Department of Agriculture, 20, 24, 50
diabetes, 25, 27–28, 41, 50, 118, 136, 138
    treatment of, 40–41
digitalis, 7, 10, 49, 94
diuretics, 31, 94–95
    thiazide, 30, 94–95
dosage form, 69, 70, 72, 75, 79–86, 91, 97
    development, 17, 75–79
drug administration
    improvement in, 17
drug approval
    processes for, 65–65
drug design, 53–54
    computer-aided (CAD), 56
drug discovery
    contribution of scientific knowledge to, 45–46
    sources for, 47, 49, 52–53
    transitions in, 19–20
drug interactions, 8, 75, 88, 93–95, 140
drug receptor, 44–45, 46, 49, 55, 56, 93, 94
drug regulation
    public influence on, 61–63
drug screening, 21–22, 31, 32, 43–44, 47, 53, 90
    tests for, 46, 47–49, 50

E

Ehrlich, Paul, 21, 47–48, 54
emphysema, 141–142
enzymes, 27, 39, 44, 45, 49, 56, 125–127, 134, 140, 141, 151, 157–158
    ACE, 45–46
    alpha-I antitrypsin, 141–142
    alteplase, 125, 126
    blockade of, 54–55
    digestive, 26–27
    plasmin, 125–126
ephedrine, 3, 49
epilepsy, 123, 124
epinephrine, 25, 54

F

familial hypercholesterolemia, 133, 138
Fleming, Alexander, 22, 32
Food and Drug Administration (FDA), 39, 65, 66–67, 70, 71, 91, 92–93, 95–96, 126, 127, 144

G

Genentech, 37–38
    success of, 41, 42
    technique developed by, 39
generics, 51, 89, 95, 96–97
gene therapy, 137, 138, 152–153
growth factors, 109, 121

H

hemophilia, 130, 131–132, 142
hepatitis, 92, 131
    hepatitis A, 104
    hepatitis B, 104, 106, 112
    hepatitis C, 112
HIV, 131, 140
hormones, 25, 37–39, 114, 127–130, 135, 141, 157–158
    growth, 37–38, 41
    thyroid, 49
human growth hormone, 41, 128, 129
Huntington's disease, 134, 138
hybridoma, 113–115, 116
hypertension, 30–32, 45
    treatment for, 30–32, 89

I

immunoglobulin, 113, 114, 116
infusion, 40, 86, 144
injection, 26, 38, 77, 86, 100, 103, 134, 141–142
insulin, 8–9, 38–39, 40, 41, 49, 57, 128, 135, 157
    isolation of, 25–28
    synthetic, 147
interferons, 109, 110–112

Investigational New Drug (IND) application, 67–70
    Treatment IND, 70
islet cells, 26–27
islets of Langerhans, 26, 40–41
Itakura, Keiichi, 37–38

J

J. Craig Venter Research Institute (JCVI), 147–148, 149, 150
Jenner, Edward, 13, 14–16, 98, 103–104, 156

L

Lister, Joseph, 12–13
lozenges, 77, 79, 80

M

marketing, 25, 44, 51, 52, 60, 61, 63
    adverse events after, 91–93
    approval for, 57, 65, 69, 96–97
    laws regulating, 61
    studies before, 64–65, 68
medicines
    in ancient civilizations, 2–4
    in the 16th and 17th centuries, 4, 6–7, 10
metabolic acidosis, 31, 32
metabolism, 25, 28, 44–45, 75, 90, 93
    of drugs, 94
monoclonal antibodies, 87,

INDEX

113, 114, 115–116
morphine, 8, 10
mutagenicity, 72
   tests for, 74

N
National Institutes of Health, 20, 36
neurogenesis, 119, 121
New Drug Application (NDA), 70–72

O
ointments, 77, 81–82
opium, 3–4, 10

P
Pacific yew, 50–52, 53
pain relief, 4, 11
Parkinson's disease, 123, 124–125
Pasteur, Louis, 13, 104
patents, 95–97, 150
   protection of, 89
penicillin, 8–9, 21, 49, 99, 100–101, 102–103, 135, 157
   discovery of, 22, 24–25
peptide therapeutics, 41, 134–136
personalized medicine, 54, 58–59, 137
pharmaceutical companies, 9, 28, 34, 45, 47, 64–65, 68, 71, 88, 89, 91, 95, 132, 155–156
   development of, 20
pharmaceutical industry, 1, 9, 22, 25, 33–34, 57
Pharmaceutical Research and Manufacturers of America (PhRMA), 88–89, 97
pharmaceuticals
   classes developed in 19th century, 18–19
   development of, 43
   research and discovery, 44–45
pharmacogenetics, 138–141
pharmacokinetic data, 68, 69, 70, 75, 93
pharmacokinetic investigations, 74–75
pharmacology, 8–9, 44, 49
   animal studies, 69, 70
pharmacopoeia, 4, 6
pharming, 137, 141–143, 146
pills, 17, 78–79, 153
plant-made pharmaceuticals (PMPs), 142–143
plasmids, 38, 39
powders, 77, 79, 85
pulmonary emboli, 126, 144

Q
quality control laboratories, 61, 63
quinine, 8, 10, 49

R
radiopharmaceuticals, 86–87
recombinant DNA technology, 28, 35–37, 41, 98, 107, 116, 135, 144–145, 147, 149,

152
regulatory agencies, 60, 61, 62, 63–65
regulatory approval, 1, 57, 60–97

S

smallpox, 13, 14–15, 16, 98, 103–104
    vaccine, 13, 156
solutions, 77, 80, 81, 86
somatostatin, 37–38
sprays, 77, 82
squill, 3–4
stem cells, 117, 120–121
    embryonic (ESCs), 120, 122–125, 154–155
    endogenous approach to therapy, 120–121
    exogenous approach to therapy, 120–121
    hematopoietic (HSCs), 123
    neural (NSCs), 119–122, 124
    research, 154–155
    sources of, 120, 154
    therapy, 99, 117–125
stroke, 30, 31, 32, 121, 123, 126, 142
    stem cell therapy used to treat, 120, 122, 123
structure-activity relationship (SAR), 54–55
suppositories, 77, 79, 80
suspensions, 77, 80, 81, 86, 103, 104
synthetic biology, 137, 146–147
    advances in, 147–151
    applications of, 151–152
syphilis, 21, 47, 48, 54

T

tablets, 76, 77–79, 83–86
    enteric coated, 78, 83
taxol, 50–52, 53
teratogenicity, 74, 90
tetracyclines, 36–37, 93, 100–101
toxicity, 2, 7, 9, 10, 12, 18–19, 33, 50, 53, 60, 63, 68, 72, 73, 75, 90, 94, 134
    studies of, 74–75
    tests for, 72–74

V

vaccines, 13, 21, 103–107, 109, 136, 141, 146, 152, 155, 156
    development of, 30
    discovery of, 12–13, 14, 16, 98
    regulation of, 66–67
vitamins, 28
    deficiencies, 28, 29
    identification of, 28–29
    thiamin (B1), 29

W

Watson, James, 34–35
World Health Organization (WHO), 64, 65